ENGLEMAN, Paul
The man with my name

S

DATE DUE

MAR 2 0 2012	

THE MAN
WITH MY NAME

ALSO BY PAUL ENGLEMAN

Dead in Center Field
Catch a Fallen Angel
Murder-in-Law
Who Shot Longshot Sam?

PAUL ENGLEMAN

ST. MARTIN'S PRESS
NEW YORK

 For information, address St. Martin's Press, 175 Fifth Avenue, New York, NY 10010.

Design by Sara Stemen

LIBRARY OF CONGRESS CATALOGING-IN-PUBLICATION DATA

Engleman, Paul.
The man with my name / Paul Engleman.
p. cm.
ISBN 0-312-09867-7
I. Title.
PS3555.N426M3 1993
813'.54—dc20 93-25961
CIP

First Edition: November 1994

10 9 8 7 6 5 4 3 2 1

For Barb, the mother of the
little man with my father's name.

The characters in this book are fictional. Any inference of similarity to actual living persons is the result of wishful thinking or paranoia on the part of the reader.

Acknowledgments

Thanks to Marc Levison for his expertise and Ed Reardon for his expert testimony. Also: Bob Campbell, Judy Duhl, Tony Judge, Keith Kahla, and Jim Trupin.

1

Frankie answers the phone because she's a light sleeper. Not like me. I could sleep through a nuclear war. Not that I'll ever have the chance. But I've slept through some ass-kicking thunderstorms over the years, and, recently, through a fire next door while Frankie was away for the weekend.

Even if the phone does wake me up, I never get out of bed to answer it. Frankie, on the other hand, she always jumps for it, no matter what time it is. She doesn't want to run the risk of missing a call from her agent.

I think this is crazy for a couple of reasons. One, her agent never calls. Two, nobody's agent calls at 3 A.M.

I can tell that's what time it is, because I'm eye-to-eye with the neon digitals on the clock radio when Frankie shakes me awake. It probably took her five minutes, but she's persistent. She's also got sharp elbows and knows all my ticklish spots.

"It's for you," she says, sticking the phone in my puss. "He says he's an old friend."

"Not anymore he ain't. Tell him to call back."

"He says it's important. He also sounds very drunk."

"Who else but a drunk would think something's important at three in the morning?" I should talk. I'm still a little drunk myself.

"Hey, Phil, you old motherfucker!"

It's a booming voice. Frankie's right. I can practically smell the booze through the phone line. I'm tempted to hang up but he'd probably just call back. Besides I'm curious to find out what he'll use for his second line.

"So . . . how the fuck are you?"

"Sleepy, real sleepy."

He laughs, a big laugh. "Oh, that's right, I'm two hours behind you."

"And ten drinks ahead of me."

He laughs again, bigger this time. "Yeah, I had a couple pops earlier." In a way, I'm glad he didn't call earlier. "I was thinking about you, so I figured, hell, why not give the little motherfucker a call."

"I can think of a reason."

"Ha, ha!" The guy's not good at taking hints. "You know how it is after you've had a few."

Now that's true, I do know that. If Frankie and I hadn't polished off a bottle of wine ourselves, I wouldn't still be talking to the guy.

"Hey, you don't sound too happy to hear from me."

I don't say anything, though I'm tempted to compliment him on his powers of perception.

"This *is* Phil Moony, right?"

"The one and only, far as I know."

"With the funny spelling?"

"Funny spelling?"

"Yeah. No E before the Y."

"I like to think of it as the correct spelling." That's a direct quote from my grandfather.

"Sure, no offense. I just want to make sure I've got the right guy."

"Sounds like you do."

"But it sounds like you don't know who this is."

"You're right. Maybe you should tell me."

"Don't you at least want to take a guess?"

His voice does sound vaguely familiar. "To be honest with you, no."

"Jesus Christ! I figured—"

"I don't know anyone by that name. At least not personally."

"Ha, ha! You still got the same old sense of humor."

"Not for much longer."

"Okay, I know, it's late out there." It's late where he is too, but I don't say anything about that. "Does the name Larry Little mean anything to you?"

I close my eyes and think for a few seconds. "Very little, I'm afraid, Larry." I'm being generous. It means nada. I know lots of people, and I've got a good memory for names. Even unmemorable names like Larry Little.

He sounds crushed. "Come on, think back, guy. Twenty years. That ain't so long ago."

"I'm thinking." I really am. Judging by the size of his voice, I figure he's a big lug. I think all the way back to high school, even though that's more than twenty years. But the only big lug that comes to mind is Tiny Cosgrove. I heard he bit the bullet back in 1980. Tiny was a cookie machine repair guy for Nabisco. He suffocated in a room full of Fig Newtons. "Sorry, Larry, I'm drawing the big blank."

"Come on, you're pulling my leg."

"You're the one that called me, Larry."

"Phil Moony on Hampton, right?"

"Hamlin." I swing my legs out from under the covers and get out of bed. Thanks to the miracle of cordless phones, I can be putting this time to productive use. I head for the bathroom.

"Yeah, that's right. Near that park up there."

"Independence Park." He's got that detail right. And he's got me totally baffled.

"Yeah, yeah, that's it. Was that Betty that answered the phone?"

"Betty?"

"You're not still married to Betty?"

That settles it. I've never even had dinner with a Betty. I've had an aversion to Bettys since sixth grade. Call it the Betty Fegley syndrome. She was bigger than Tiny Cosgrove.

"I hate to tell you this, Larry, but you've got the wrong Phil

Moony." Actually I'm rather pleased about it. But I am surprised to learn there's another Phil Moony. With that spelling, we're probably cousins.

His voice gets real quiet. "Ah, shit, don't tell me." He sounds devastated. "I'm sorry, mister."

"You can call me Phil." I figure that might cheer him up a bit. Why I would want to cheer up a drunk who calls in the middle of the night, I don't know. I guess I'm more drunk than I thought.

"Yeah, that's right, Phil. I'm sorry, Phil. I really am. Me and the other Phil, we used to be business partners in the late sixties. Had a nightclub on Rush Street, but it didn't fly. It was my club actually. Phil, he was just the silent partner."

He'd have to be. I doubt he could've gotten a word in edgewise.

"So how's the weather in the Windy City? Damn I miss that town."

"It's freezing."

"Ha, ha! I don't miss that. I'm in L.A. now. Orange County, actually."

"What was the name of your club?" Why am I asking?

"I doubt you'd remember it. It's probably had fifty fucking names since then."

"Try me." Moving into the living room, I pick a cigarette out of Frankie's pack. I don't smoke anymore. At least I stopped smoking my brand.

"The Purple Haze."

"Sounds vaguely familiar." I'm lying. For some reason, I feel sorry for this guy. Frankie says I'm a soft touch. After eight years, she's still unsure whether it's because I've got a big heart or a small brain.

"I guess you wouldn't have any way of knowing where the other Phil lives."

"Until two minutes ago, I didn't know there was another one. Unless . . ."

"Unless *what?*" He sounds hopeful. Too hopeful, considering what I'm about to tell him.

"Nothing. I just realized it's probably because of him that I get all this weird mail." Up to now, I'd figured it was someone on the fire department or the police department playing a joke on me. I used to work for the fire department.

"Like what do you get?"

"Junk mail. Offers for grow lights, books on growing pot, magazines like *High Times*, *Sinsemilla Tips*. Stuff like that."

"Yeah, that sounds like old Phil all right."

Old Phil sounds like a guy I wouldn't mind knowing. I'm not much of a dope smoker myself, but Frankie loves the stuff. She says it helps her write and these days it's getting real hard to find.

"That's pretty amazing, the two of you living on the same street and all."

"It's a small world."

"Yeah, you're telling me." He pauses. "You sure that wasn't Betty?"

"Positive."

"Man, it sure sounded like her."

"You want me to check the phone book, see if there's another listing?" I'm certain there isn't, but it's the least I can do.

"Sure, if you don't mind. I mean you're probably getting ready to go to bed, aren't you?"

"To be honest with you Larry, it's almost time to get up."

"Jeez, I guess it's later than I thought."

I check the book. There are two numbers, but just as I thought, they're both mine. My office and my home. Frankie's home, actually. She owns it. I just live here.

"Sorry, Larry, you're S.O.L."

"Huh?"

"Shit out of luck."

"Damn." Larry sounds truly bummed.

"You want to give me your number in case I run into him?"

"Hell yeah, you got a pencil?"

"Just a good head for numbers. Shoot."

He gives me a number with a 213 area code. I'm just drowsy enough to forget it, so I write it on one of the note pads that Frankie keeps stationed around the house.

"Damn. I really need to talk to that son of a bitch."

"How bad?"

"Real bad."

"Well, maybe I can find him for you."

"Really, you think so?"

"That all depends on how hard I try. And how hard I try depends on how much it's worth to you."

"It'd be worth plenty, believe me. It'd be worth even more to Phil, if he knew what I had to tell him."

"Great. How does five hundred bucks sound?"

"What? Do you do this for a living or something?"

"Yeah. Or something." I don't see any point in telling Larry that the only missing person I've ever found was an Irish setter. But I know I can do it. And it just so happens I'm looking for something to do right now.

"What are you, a private investigator?"

"Not officially. I don't have a license, and the state won't give me one."

"Why not?"

"Tell me how five hundred sounds, then maybe I'll tell you."

"I'm sorry. I didn't mean to pry. Five hundred's just fine. It'd be worth twice that, easy. I mean, if you found him."

"Fine. Make it a grand then."

"Ha ha! You're a funny son of a bitch, Phil. I was only kidding. But I'm sure the other Phil would pay. He's always had the bucks."

"What exactly does the other Phil do?"

"All kinds of shit. At least he used to. Nowadays, I don't know. But I'm sure he's doing okay for himself. Phil's one of those guys that always managed to land on their feet, if you know what I mean."

"Yeah, I know exactly what you mean." Not like me. I'm a headfirst type.

"So. Why won't those pricks let you have a license?"

I yawn as I watch the numerals on the clock roll over to 4:00. The answer to Larry's question would be a very long story. I give him the short version.

"Politics."

"Fuck. Tell me about it. Everything in Chi is politics."

He's got that one right.

"So tell me what I'm supposed to tell Phil Moony," I say.

"You sound pretty sure you're going to find him."

"Having a positive attitude's fifty percent of the job, Lar."

He lets out a laugh, but they're getting smaller. It sounds like the booze is wearing off and he's finally winding down. Suddenly his voice gets very low, almost a whisper.

"Tell him to call me right away, okay? But make sure you tell him I saw Tony Rio."

"Rio?"

"Yeah. Spelled just like the city in Chile."

"Brazil."

"Same difference. Tell him Rio got back from vacation early and he's looking for him. Okay?"

"Am I to take it that the other Phil was hoping Rio would be away on vacation a lot longer?"

"Trust me, Phil, more than that you don't want to know. Adios, amigo. If I ever get back to Chi, I'll buy you a beer."

"And if I ever get out to L.A., I'll buy you a wine cooler."

He lets out a chuckle. It sounds like the last one he's got left. "Say hi to Betty, will you?"

2

I pause in the doorway and watch the morning sunshine light up the faint cluster of freckles that straddles Frankie's nose and blankets her cheeks. It's a lovely sight. I should stay up all night more often.

"Good morning, sleeping beauty." I'm holding a cup of coffee and the *Sun-Times*, open to the obits, which is the first section she reads. I've got my jacket on.

She gives her eyes a complete working-over with both hands before saying anything. It could be that she's especially sleepy today. More likely, she's astonished to see me parked bedside.

"What's going on? What time is it?"

"Seven-thirty. You look like you've seen a ghost."

She yawns and takes the coffee. "It's nothing. I just had this weird dream that you got up before I did."

"Maybe you weren't dreaming."

She puts the coffee down on the night table, then punches the pillow on my side of the bed. "Yeah, you're right. Maybe I wasn't. What's the occasion?"

I shrug. "It's the first day of the rest of my life. I want to get a good jump on it."

She pulls herself to a sitting position, and her slender shoulders slide out the neck of her sleeping shirt. Frankie doesn't wear pajamas or a nightgown, just my old T-shirts. She's a size four, I'm a 44.

"After your phone call last night, I expected you to sleep all day. Who was that guy?"

"His name was Larry Little. He had the wrong number."

"Are you kidding? That has to be the longest wrong number in the history of phone conversations. It seemed like you were talking all night."

"It seemed like it to me too. He had the wrong number, but it turned out he had the right name."

"Your name?"

I nod.

"Same spelling?"

I nod again.

Frankie's brow furrows as she takes my hand. "Darling, I'm so sorry. I thought your name was unique. Like mine."

"That's all right, I'll get over it in a few years. And what makes you think your name's unique? I'll bet there's dozens of Frank Martins in Chicago."

"Yeah, sure." Frankie brushes back silky black strands that have fallen across her eyes. "But how much do you want to bet any of them are named Francesca?"

"I stopped betting with you a long time ago. You never pay off when you lose." I kiss her hand, lifting it with me as I get up.

"Where are you going?"

"To the office."

"Already?" She tugs at my sleeve as I start to turn away. "Phil, I hope you're not rushing out because of what I said yesterday."

I shake my head. "What'd you say yesterday?"

"You remember. About you not keeping up your end of the arrangement?"

"Oh yeah, that."

The arrangement is a bit complicated to explain. Basically it comes down to this. I haven't had a real job for two years now. And to be perfectly honest, I don't really want one. Which is just fine with Frankie. It's just that she doesn't want me hanging around the house all day. That's because she doesn't have a job either. And she likes having the whole place to herself.

Seeing how the house was left to us by Frankie's father when he died last year, it seems only fair that she gets to be the one who stays home. My dad left us his Chrysler LeBaron when he died, and I'm the one that drives it. Besides, it's not like Frankie's sitting around doing nothing, although, come to think of it, she never misses "Oprah" or "People's Court."

Frankie's working on a novel. It's her second. The first one hasn't been sold yet, but it will be, any day now. At least that's what we're hoping. It was real good. This one's going to even better, judging by the ten pages she let me read.

Before she became a novelist, Frankie was a reporter for the *Sun-Times*. And a good one. I should know. I turned her on to some of her best stories.

As for myself, I'm no slouch either. At least I didn't used to be. I put in twelve years as a field paramedic with the Chicago Fire Department. When you do that you've got lots of free time, because you work twenty-four hours on, forty-eight hours off. But after the twenty-four hours on, you *know* you've been working, believe me.

There are two main differences between my situation and Frankie's. She quit her job, I got canned from mine. She knows what she wants to do, I don't have the slightest idea.

That's not true exactly. I've got lots of ideas. The problem is, they all sound pretty good to me. For about a week.

I've thought about working at a hospital, of course, or teaching first aid. I tried both of those, in fact, and I gave up real fast. Too many hours under fluorescent lights give me a pounding headache. I've thought about driving a cab, because I like to drive and I know the city, but that sounds like a good way to get shot or knifed and a bad way to make any money. I've thought about being a schoolteacher, but that sounds like an even better way to get shot or knifed and an even worse way to make any money. I've considered sales, marketing, computers, cars, fruits, vegetables, retail, wholesale. You name it, I've thought about it. I've even flirted with the idea of going back to school—med school maybe, or law school. But it turns out that costs two arms and two legs instead of just one of each like I thought.

Lately I've been toying with the notion of hiring myself out as an accident investigator to lawyers or insurance companies. I can scope out an accident scene with the best of them. But I hate lawyers and insurance companies, so the only way that would provide any satisfaction is if I could gouge them big time. But they're the masters of gouging, so who am I fooling?

My strategy—and Frankie's all in favor of it—is to stay patient. One of these days, I just know it, some really great idea is going to walk up and bite me on the nose. Until then I'm just biding my time, getting my feet wet in this and that. Fortunately, I can afford to be choosy. I'm not supposed to say a word about this, but I got a handsome little going-away present when I left the fire department. In their lexicon of bureaucratic doublespeak, it's called severance pay. In plain English, it's called hush money. When they decided to bring the axe down on me, I decided to call their bluff. And it worked.

There's no record of it. Nobody knows about it, not even the IRS. Which is why I'd be a fool to say anything.

Anyway, as far as the arrangement Frankie and I have goes, I'm supposed to leave the house by nine-thirty each day so she can get started writing. She doesn't care where I go, and I don't always tell her. Most days I go to my office, but sometimes I just drive around the city, watching people, thinking about things. Neither of us is what you'd call a morning person, so we don't follow the rule to the letter. But I'm on my way out the door by ten, never fail. That's when "Oprah" comes on, and by then I'm always hungry.

The arrangement works fine most days, but every once in a while the system breaks down. When that happens, there's a lot of screaming, and most of it is Frankie screaming at me. The stuff she screams sounds so similar each time that if you taped it and played it back you wouldn't be able to tell which was Frankie and which was Memorex.

It always comes down to the same question: Why am I content to sit around like a mope instead of doing something useful with my life?

It's a good question, even if I don't always appreciate the

spirit in which it's asked. And it seems like I've always got the same answer: I must have a low threshold of contentment. That's not an answer Frankie's usually content with.

Yesterday was a breakdown day. They don't come all that often, but frequently enough that I can shake off the effects pretty quickly. By the time I get to the office, I've usually forgotten about it. If it's a particularly nasty one, I might stop by Sullivan's for a couple fingers of skull-popper on the way.

Not Frankie. She's a brooder. When we fight in the morning, it stays with her all day long. She's usually the one on the attack, so she feels guilty for the things she's said. When Frankie gets mad, she says some pretty mean things. But a lot of it's because both of her parents drank like fish. As a rule, kids of alcoholics blame themselves for stuff that goes wrong. Frankie's no exception to it. She's always the first to apologize or take the blame for things.

And I'm not above letting her do it.

Breakdown days almost always get resolved the same way. We don't talk to each other all day. Without any planning, Frankie cooks a real nice dinner, something that takes hours to prepare, like lasagna with artichoke hearts or lobster risotto. I come home armed with flowers and a couple of bottles of good wine. Sometimes I rent a couple of videos—a romantic tear-jerker for me to suffer through and a low-budget actioner to make Frankie's skin crawl. I have this theory that watching these together is a celebration of our differences. It brings us closer.

When I first get in the door, we both pretend nothing's wrong. We exchange kisses on the cheeks with all the passion of conventioneers trading business cards. I make a point of sounding casual as I mention the flowers and scout for a vase. She uses the same tone when she announces the dinner menu. It isn't until after I open the wine that we finally break the ice. We have a perfunctory toast—"cheers" from me or "*cin cin*" from her—then eye each other from short range as we drink.

This is the waiting game, wondering which one of us will give in and apologize first. There's really no suspense in it, because Frankie's always the one who does it. I let her do it because I know she needs to do it.

Plus there's this little problem I have with not being able to do it.

As soon as Frankie blurts the first one out, the apologies start flying fast and furious. It becomes a full-blown apology orgy for the duration of the evening. We do it over appetizers, between bites of the main course, all through coffee and dessert. I've even been known to pause the VCR right in the middle of the chase scene and apologize. By the time our heads hit the pillows, things are back to our normal state of bliss.

Just the same, for the next two weeks or so, I make a point of being out the door by nine-thirty. And for another day or so, Frankie still has to work off some residual guilt. That's what she's doing now.

She pulls me close and begins to stare me down with those big mahogany eyes. "I really didn't mean all those things I said yesterday, Phil."

I nod. "Of course you didn't."

"God, I can't believe what a bitch I was."

"I know. Neither can I." I grin as I say that. Otherwise I'd be dead meat.

She lunges at me with fists clenched, but I put up my arms to fend off the blows while mounting my retreat. For an instant she thinks about chasing me down, but instead she flops back into bed and pulls up the covers. Frankie's no dummy.

I wave from the doorway. "I'd love to stay home and wrestle, darling, but I'm a busy guy with lots of busy-guy things to do."

"Such as?"

"Such as doing the job Larry Little hired me to do."

"Who?"

"Our late-night caller. Have you forgotten already?"

"*He* hired you? To do *what*?"

"He wants me to find the other man with my name."

"How much is he paying you?" Leave it to Frankie to cut right to the chase.

"We didn't really get into that."

I don't make a habit of lying to Frankie. But if I told her Larry Little agreed to $500, she'd immediately suspect he was involved in something illegal.

And of course, there'd be a 99.9 percent chance she'd be right.

Some guys get awfully sentimental about their old buddies—especially drunken guys—but I've never known any to harbor sentiments that go that far down into their pockets. Admittedly, Larry hadn't forked over any dough. But I'd get him to put his money where his mouth was before I opened mine. And his message about Tony Rio clearly made it more than a social call. You could be sure the "vacation" Rio was returning from hadn't been booked through a regular travel agent.

Frankie is deathly afraid of me running afoul of the law again. I appreciate her concern, of course, but it's almost gotten to the point where she gets anxious when I drive over 55. I tell her the cops in town all have bigger agendas than making my life miserable. Not that I completely discount her belief that I'm at least a minor agenda item on their daily grudge sheets.

The way I look at it, if I get in trouble again, I can't lose my job. That's because this time I don't have a job to lose. There'd be some publicity, I'm sure. But with Frankie's father dead, it wouldn't embarrass him like last time. If the truth be told, I didn't mind my fifteen minutes in the spotlight.

As far as real trouble goes, there's no way I'd ever get involved in something bad enough that I'd end up doing time. The prisons are too overbooked to have openings for guys like me.

"Finding this guy might not be as easy as you think," Frankie says.

"What makes you think I think it's going to be easy?"

She smiles. "Sweetheart, you don't do anything you think's going to be hard."

"That's not true. What about remodeling the basement?"

"I did that." She swings her legs out from under the covers and gets out of bed, all in one motion.

"I helped."

"You *watched*."

She starts to yawn, tries to stifle it with her hand, but it's a losing battle. She gives in, letting her arms spread into a full court stretch. She's framed in the sunlight.

As she leans her head back, I can see the shiny ends of her black hair dusting her shoulders. I admire that view, not saying anything.

My silence throws her. She stops abruptly and zeros in on me. "I didn't hurt your feelings, did I?"

"Mortally." For a moment, she's not sure if I'm serious. I hold my poker face as long as I can.

She advances on me, shaking her head sheepishly. Frankie hates to be caught in a moment of gullibility. Suddenly her voice is all business.

"Now the first thing you need to do is find out the guy's last Chicago address. I'd suggest you go to the—"

"Would you like me to stay home and write your novel for you today?"

She stops, hands on hips, and glowers. It's good-natured glowering. Frankie loves to run my life, but she hates to be caught doing it.

"I deserved that," she says.

"You deserve everything you get from me."

"That's because you give me so damn little."

"I'll gladly give you a damn phone call if I need your help. How's that?"

"Splendid, just splendid."

It's splendid with me too. The fact is, I don't know the first thing about finding a missing person. But I'm confident I can figure out how to do it. Especially if Frankie's willing to help. This sort of thing is right up her alley.

She opens her arms, inviting me inside them for a visit. I accept and she administers a brief but hearty hero's sendoff. Next to her patented hero's welcome, this is probably my favorite thing in the whole world. Then I'm off to the office.

My office is right on Logan Square, where Milwaukee Avenue crosses Kedzie and Logan boulevards. I picked it for three basic reasons: location, atmosphere, price.

It's only three El stops down the Northwest line from our house. When I got it, I figured I'd hop on the CTA during the winter and walk the two miles or so during warm weather. For two years now, I've driven every day. But I've still got the option of taking the train or walking any time I want.

As far as atmosphere goes, I figure any neighborhood where you see *Cerveza Fria* signs hanging next door to places with names like *Droszka Karzckma*, you know things will never get too dull.

The building is an ancient three-story walkup that once upon a time formed a perfect right triangle. The sagging, scarred legs of the triangle face Logan on the north and Kedzie on the west. Its hypotenuse is the back side of the building, which runs the length of the alley behind the Banco Popular de Puerto Rico.

The tip of the triangle points directly to Logan Square, which is actually a circle. At the center of the circle is a four-sided stairway leading up to a white marble monument. The monument is a towering obelisk, not quite the stature of the Washington monument in D.C., but impressive just the same.

At the top of the obelisk sits an American eagle. At the bottom of it, on most afternoons and evenings, sit groups of teenagers. I've heard them refer to the monument as "the turkey." I don't think many of them are headed for college. Most of them are armed with tools for tagging. I suspect some of them are armed with more dangerous weapons. I'm positive some of them are dealing drugs.

None of them has ever bothered me. I've never seen them bother anyone else.

Of all the tenants in the building, I've got the best seat in the house. A top-floor cubicle on the point of the triangle overlooking the park. Standing on my desk, I'm almost eye-to-eye with the eagle. By bending down real low, I can see half a block up Milwaukee Avenue, past the blood bank, the liquor store, and the billboard with the Virgin Mary's 800 number on it. On a clear day I can see all the way to the clothing store that specializes in "styles to fit your wallet."

In addition to the view, the two windows provide cross ventilation, which is a must in the summer. There's no air-conditioning, so the only relief from the heat comes from portable fans. I've got three of them. It took some doing, but I've learned how to adjust them to effectively neutralize the fumes from Ronnie's Grill, the 24-hour greasy spoon that sits directly below. On really hot afternoons when the sun turns the building into a broiling pan, I've also been known to slip out to the Mexican restaurant across the park and siesta on margaritas.

All this for the unbelievably low price of $275 a month.

My landlord, Jerry, hasn't raised the rent, and he promises he won't until he's done rehabbing the building. I figure I've got until the end of the century. Jerry has big plans but a small bankroll. He tells me I'm his best tenant. That's not saying very much.

On the ground floor, there's a dry cleaner called Ruby's that's no longer owned by Ruby, a newspaper shop that still carries *Look* magazine and a beeper store with a security system that requires customers to be buzzed in. The beeper guy is the only one who seems to be doing much business. Most of his customers look to be about sixteen. He looks at least twenty-one.

On the second floor is a Polish podiatrist whose name I can't pronounce. His sign has a translation under his profession for those who are confused by long words: FOOTS DOCTOR. Next door to him is a psychic reader named Madame Yvetta. I've never had the pleasure of crossing paths with her, either, but I've heard she's good at what she does. While waiting for coffee in Ronnie's one morning, I overheard a geezer in a Notre Dame cap telling someone she had put him in touch with the ghost of Knute Rockne. Rockne grew up in this neighborhood.

There are a few other tenants on the second floor, but I have no idea what they do. I suspect they either like it that way or they have something to hide. Of course I should talk. I'm sure nobody has any idea what goes on behind the frosted glass door on the third floor with the hand-lettered sign that says MOONY ENTERPRISES—World Headquarters. I suspect anybody who's seen it thinks it has something to do with Reverend Sun Myung Moon. They probably duck when they hear me coming, expecting me to sell them flowers.

That's what Artie the Artist thought before he worked up the nerve to knock and find out. Artie's the only other guy on the third floor. I don't know his last name. He's only been there three months. Before that I had the whole floor to myself.

Artie told me he was in graphic arts, but I've got this nagging suspicion he's an undercover cop. When I mentioned my suspicions to Frankie, she threw a fit and insisted I find another office. But I think she's really being paranoid to think Artie's keeping tabs on me. I figure he's got his eye on the beeper or the turkey.

Artie was relieved to find out I wasn't a Moonie. He told me his sister took up with one and ended up getting married in Madison Square Garden. He got real pissed off when he talked about it. If I *had* been a Moonie, I think he might have hit me. That would have been big trouble, because Artie's a big guy. Bigger than any artist I've ever met, not that I've met that many.

I'd say he's got three inches and twenty-five pounds on me. Rounding up, I'm six feet, two hundred.

I park my car next to the church where Knute Rockne used to be an altar boy. I'm told it's the oldest Norwegian church in the city. A chilly mist hangs heavy in the air, covering the square like a wet gray blanket. It's classic drab March weather for Chicago. But it feels like a reprieve because it's still February. The square is deserted as I stroll across it, and the boulevards have a peaceful quality as they wait for the city to wake up.

Chicago's boulevards were modeled after the boulevards of Paris. On mornings like these, I almost feel like I'm in Paris. I imagine myself in a café on the Left Bank, knocking back shots of espresso and eating a hot croissant. Then I go into Ronnie's and get a jelly donut.

Life is sweet, but it ain't that sweet.

4

I get right to work. I don't even allow myself a peek at the sports section. Well, maybe just a little peek, while I'm prying the lid off my Styrofoam coffee cup. Ronnie's doesn't have the right size lids, so they put them on upside down. I had to weather a few coffee storms before mastering the technique for prying them off.

I rock back on my chair and contemplate my first move. If Frankie were doing this, she'd know right where to start. But I can't call her for advice just yet. There's some male pride and ego at stake here. Plus who knows? Maybe I'll learn something.

Frankie would go about this in an orderly fashion. I'm just playing my hunches. That's kind of odd, because when it comes to work, I'm usually the methodical one and she tends to be impulsive.

It seems to me that many of the people who move out of Chicago move to the suburbs. I call directory assistance in area code 708 and ask for the listing. I start to give the operator a song-and-dance number about how I don't know the address, just the name. Before I can finish spitting out my excuse, she has me patched into a tape: "The number you have requested is unlisted at the customer's request. No further information is available."

I listen to it all the way through one more time. This is out of habit. I like this woman's voice. I sometimes wonder if I'm the only guy in Chicago who does.

I dial info again, and this time I'm ready. "I'm calling long distance and I'm looking for two numbers," I say. This should put an actual living operator at my disposal for a few seconds at least. "The first listing is for Moony, M-O-O-N-Y. First name Phil, P-H-I-L. I think it's in Bensenville."

This is just a guess. Bensenville is a perfunctory strip of topless bars and cheap motels just one courtesy-van stop south of O'Hare. It's the kind of place where a guy who owned a Rush Street club named Purple Haze in the sixties might end up in the nineties. I've never known anyone who lives in Bensenville. I'm not sure it actually has residents.

"Checking for Moony," she says. Her tone is clipped. A moment later she assures me that she's still checking.

I tell her I believe her and advise her to take her time. That doesn't stop her from repeating "Still checking" like a mantra every three seconds. I imagine some lug of a supervisor with bad breath and a bad rug standing over her with a stopwatch.

"I have no listing for Moony in Bensenville."

"Maybe it's in Rosemont." That's the next town north, an asphalt jumble abutting the airport runways. I wonder how many guesses she's going to allow me.

"There's one in Winnetka."

"Yes, *that's* right. Winnetka."

I can almost hear surprise in her silence. Not even a Martian would get Bensenville and Rosemont confused with Winnetka. It's like the difference between creamed chipped beef and chateaubriand. If he's living in Winnetka, the other Phil Moony must be doing pretty well for himself. Better than me at least.

"That number is . . . *unlisted*," she says slowly.

I imagine the color draining from her face as the data unfolds on her computer terminal. She's been outfoxed and she knows it. If a supervisor is monitoring, she'll probably receive demerits for volunteering confidential information. I don't gloat. It's the system's fault, not hers. Her secret's safe with me.

I ask her for the street address. She says she can't give that out, adding, "You know that."

Yes I do. But you can't blame a guy for trying.

I'm feeling pretty smug as I hang up. Two phone calls and I

know Phil Moony's hometown. I try directory assistance a third time, hoping it will be the charm. It's not. Even on a fourth effort, I can't cajole the street address out of an operator. I guess I'll have to work to get that.

I dial our number at home. When Frankie picks up, I say I just called to tell her I love her.

"Sure you did. What's the real reason?"

"You don't believe me."

"I wouldn't believe you if you were strapped to a stack of Bibles with a stick of dynamite up your ass."

"Baby, you're killing me with this romantic talk. What's the matter? Am I interrupting an important show?"

"I don't even have the TV on. I'm trying to work. How about you? Made any progress in your search for Mr. Moony?"

"A little." I try to sound nonchalant. "I know what town he lives in."

"Already? I figured you'd still be reading the papers around now."

"You underestimate my determination in the face of a challenge."

"Well I'm sorry, I'll never do it again. So where does he live?"

"All's forgiven. In Winnetka. But his number's unlisted and I don't know the address."

"That's easy enough to find out. Just go downtown and check the property tax files. The assessor's office has them, so does the clerk's office."

"Downtown?"

"You could call. But it'll probably take longer for someone to answer the phone. And chances are they won't tell you anything anyway."

"But why would I go downtown, if Moony lives in Winnetka?"

"Because they're county records. And the last I heard, Winnetka was still in Cook County. Unless you've heard something different. Have you?"

"You know me. As far as I'm concerned, north of the city limits, it's all Wisconsin."

"Yes, I know. And west of the city is all Iowa. Can you imagine how insufferable you'd be if you were a New Yorker?"

That's something to think about, but right now I can't, because there's someone knocking on my door.

"I've got to go," I tell Frankie. "Someone's here to see me."

"Who is it?"

Peering through the frosted glass, I can make out the outline of a red jacket. "I think it's Artie the Artist." He wears a Blackhawks jacket every day, which makes him the only artist I've ever met who likes hockey. He's also the only hockey fan I've ever met who wears an earring. It's a gold hoop on a chain, with a black puck in the middle of it. His girlfriend designs jewelry. She made it for him.

"You mean Artie the narc, don't you?" Sometimes I think that if it weren't for me, Frankie wouldn't have any friends. She's too inclined to think the worst of people. "Whatever you do, don't let him in."

"I love you," I say. "I'll call you later."

By the time I hang up, I have to step out into the hall and call Artie back. He turns slowly, lumbers toward me and thrusts out his paw. "Hey dude, what's happenin'?"

For some reason, this question always throws me off. I never know what to say. You can't say you're fine because the question isn't how you are or how you're doing. I almost always end up shrugging and saying, "Nothing much."

I invite Artie in, and he makes himself right at home. He goes straight for my swivel chair, leans back and does a full revolution. I look on a bit nervously. I just got the damn thing fixed.

"Man, you sure got a great view in here. Not like me. I'm stuck in the crack of the building's ass."

"A real shithole, would you say?"

"You got it." He grins and holds his hand up for a high five. I give it a perfunctory tap.

I've never been in Artie's office. It's located on the opposite side of the building. As far as I can recall, the only time he's been in mine was that once when he wanted to find out if I was a Sun Myung Moony. We talk when we run into each other on the stairs or in the can. Usually about hockey. Artie has season tickets, and he keeps saying he's going to take me to a game. But it's not like we're friends. So it's pretty unusual that he's come to visit.

"Tonight, dude," he says, holding out his hand. It's got a pair of tickets in it. "They're playing Detroit. Should be a great game. Lots of fights."

"Great," I say as I take the tickets from his outstretched hand. I think it's strange that there are never any paint stains on it. If the truth be told, I'm really not all that interested in going to a game. I've just been saying I'd like to go whenever Artie's mentioned it, because I figured he'd never get around to formally asking me. "But what about you?" I ask.

"Nah, I can't go. I wish I could. I gotta go out to the Apple." Artie's the only guy I know who still calls New York the Big Apple. Maybe the only guy I know who ever did.

"Well, let me pay you for them at least." I pull out my wallet.

Artie grins. When he does that, his cheeks rise, and his eyes seem to dip beneath them, like a pair of sunsets. "Yeah, that's the general idea, dude."

I sneak a peek at the price on one of the tickets. Thirty bucks! No wonder I haven't been to a game in years. I thought it was too expensive back then.

"They're great seats," he says. "Fourth-row mezz."

They better be. I nod as I dip into my singles supply to come up with sixty. I'll have to stop at the Banco Popular on my way to lunch.

"I've got a favor to ask you."

"What's that?" I don't tell him I just did one for him.

He holds out a ring with three keys on it. "Would you pick up my mail while I'm gone and put it in my office? I'm expecting some checks and I don't want to miss them."

"Sure. How long are you going to be gone?"

"That all depends."

He doesn't say exactly what it depends on and I don't ask.

He gets up, stretches and reties the bandana on his forehead. "Do you smoke dope, man?"

"No." I blurt it out reflexively, and it comes out sounding like I think it will shrink your pecker. I try to correct the impression. "I mean I used to, but not anymore."

Artie nods. "I was just wondering. 'Cause I was going to say, if you do, there's a bag of weed in the bottom right drawer of my desk. Feel free to roll yourself a doob if you want."

"Thanks a lot. Maybe I will."

We shake as he exits. I tell him to have a nice trip, he tells me to have a great game.

I decide to take the El to the Loop and hit the assessor's office before lunch. I'm on my way out the door when the phone rings.

I consider leaving it for my message machine to handle. It's probably someone calling with a job offer. I get lots of job offers. When you know how to save lives and people are dying off in record numbers, that alone makes you very employable. Plus I've got quite a few people looking out for me. A lot of guys believe I did the right thing. They think I got screwed. Of course there are some guys who'd like to rip off my head and shit down my neck. I figure it's about two to one, friends to head-rippers.

It's Frankie. She's one of the friends, of course, but right now, she's in a head-ripping frame of mind. I can tell because I don't get any hello, how are you, it's me, or anything like that. She launches right into message mode.

"Another damn weirdo just called here looking for you."

"What do you mean, *another*?"

"Remember last night—Sam Small or whatever his name was?"

"Larry Little."

"Yes, that's right. Well, you just got another one."

"Did he say what his name was?"

"Yes he did. Tony Rio. And he sounds like a real asshole."

"What makes you say that?"

"Because he kept calling me Betty and he asked if I still had cute little tennis-ball tits."

"What did you tell him?"

"I said my name wasn't Betty and it wasn't any of his damn business what my tits look like. And then I asked if he was the same Tony Rio who had the world's smallest cock."

"And what did he say to that?"

"He laughed and said I hadn't changed one bit."

"You haven't. You're still the same old Betty."

"Who the hell's Betty? What's going on, Phil?"

"She's the other Moony's wife. It's him that Tony Rio's looking for. Not me. It's just that he doesn't know it."

"Well, he's in Chicago and he thinks it's you he's looking for. He said he had something to give you. He said you'd know what it was all about. But you don't, right?"

"Actually I do, sort of."

"Do you want to tell me?"

"Not now. I'll know more after I talk to Rio. Did he leave a number?"

"Yes. Two-oh-two, one-six-two-nine. And I gave him yours at the office. But I wanted to call and warn you first."

"Thanks. That was thoughtful of you."

"I'm always thoughtful, you know that."

"Yeah, but it's always nice to be reminded."

"In that case, can I ask you a question?"

"Sure, go ahead."

"Are you sure you know what you're doing?"

"Darling, I never have any idea what I'm doing. You know that."

"I'm *serious*, Phil."

"I'm not. I'm just going to call Rio and tell him it's a case of mistaken identity but I know how to find the guy he's looking for. And for that I'm going to make a little money. Sounds easy."

"Too easy. If you ask me, it sounds like trouble with a capital T."

"You know what, Frankie?"

"I know, I know. Nobody asked me."

5

"Yo!"

It's not much to go on, but the voice at the other end of the line doesn't sound very friendly. Maybe Frankie's prejudices have rubbed off on me. Or maybe it's that even in one syllable I can detect equal parts sandpaper and grain alcohol.

"Tony Rio?" I ask.

"The one and only."

I wish I could say that. Under the circumstances, I guess I don't really mind another guy having my name.

"Is this Moony?"

"Yeah, but I'm not the guy you think I am."

"You never were."

The guy's got a sense of humor. That surprises me.

"No, seriously," I say. "My name's Phil Moony, but I'm not the Phil Moony you're looking for."

"Moony with no E, right?"

"Yeah, that's right."

"Live on Hamlin?"

"Yeah, but—"

"Then you're the guy I'm looking for."

"No I'm not."

"How do you know?"

"Because I'm not married to Betty. How's that?"

He lets out a chuckle. At first I think he's clearing his throat. "That's your tough fuckin' luck, is what that is."

"Listen, Tony, I've already been through all this with a friend of yours."

"A friend of mine? Who?"

"Larry Little."

"Who says he's my friend? Did he tell you that?"

"Not in so many words."

"What else did he tell you?"

"Not much. He called my house by mistake, same as you did. He said you were looking for the other Moony. He said you'd been away on vacation."

"Ha! Yeah, that's right, I've been on vacation. And I've got a little souvenir for Moony. You know where he lives?"

"No. But I think I might be able to find him."

"Then we should talk. You know where to find me?"

"No."

"The Milshire Hotel."

"On Milwaukee Avenue?"

"Yeah, that's right."

"Jesus."

"What? You know the place?"

I most certainly do and I'd be willing to bet I'm one of the few people in Chicago who does. That's because it's only half a block from my building. I can't see it from my office, but I'd bet Artie has a bird's-eye view of it from his.

The Milshire is your basic no-frills neighborhood flophouse. Not the sort of place that draws out-of-town businessmen. Unless they've got appointments with hookers. I'm not sure it even attracts many of them. That kind of action's more suited to places near the Loop. At the Milshire, I doubt they take Visa and I'm sure they don't have smoke alarms. I'm surprised they have phones in the rooms.

"How did you come to pick such a fine place?"

"I didn't. Someone picked it for me."

"Are you enjoying the accommodations?"

"It's beauteous, just fuckin' beauteous. I take it you know how to get here?"

"I could spit there from here."

"Don't try it. I've got my window open. Room two-fourteen."

As soon as I hang up, it occurs to me that it's not such a smart idea to meet a guy who sounds as mean as Tony Rio in a place that looks as seedy as the Milshire. It might be smarter to have Rio come to my office. I think about calling him back and suggesting that, but I decide that if he is a bad dude, the last thing I want is for him to know where my office is.

I tell myself I'm being paranoid. Living with Frankie can have that effect. When I was working, I used to go into places ten times as sleazy as the Milshire. In fact, I used to get off on being in dangerous places and situations. Of course then I had an advantage. With most people, the instant they see your white uniform, they treat you with respect. Some of them regard you with awe. In street clothes, you're just another nobody.

On my way down the stairs, I tell myself nothing bad is going to happen in the middle of the day. I try to focus on the notion that I'm actually going to earn some money for a change. But as I step out into the damp chill and turn down the alley off Kedzie, I know that money has nothing to do with it. That's just a rationalization. The real motivation is curiosity. This is an invitation to follow the unknown, to find out where something will lead to. It's a chance to take a chance for a change. That's something I don't get to do anymore. When it comes right down to it, I've been bored ever since they canned my ass.

I pause outside the Milshire and look back up the street at my building. I can make out the window of Artie's office but I can't see into it. Even though the sky is overcast, the reflection of the muted sunlight on the pane blocks the view.

Inside, the lobby of the hotel is dark and cramped. I've been in so many buildings that smell like this over the years that there's a sense of familiarity almost pleasing about it. But there's nothing pleasant about the smell itself. It hits like a punch in the nose, a state of staleness so advanced that all the odors seem to have conspired to suck the oxygen out of the air.

I have to pause a moment for my eyes to adjust. I breathe through my mouth. I can make out the reception desk a few steps ahead under the glow of a bare bulb that's 60 watts, tops. As I lean against the desk, I notice a hand-lettered sign in English and Spanish that says the clerk will be back in five minutes.

I don't see any point in waiting. I turn and scan for the stairs. As I do, I hear a small voice say, "Up?"

I'm startled, but I manage to nod as the outline of a thin man sitting in a chair comes into view. He's pointing at a door a few yards to my right. I mumble thanks as I turn the knob, then start up the creaky steps.

The stairway is twice as bright as the lobby, thanks to a pair of bulbs. The door leading to the second floor is open, and the window shades are up at both ends of the narrow hallway, permitting daylight to seep in. The wallpaper and carpet are matching shades of brown that make you wonder if someone wasn't trying to see how depressing they could make the place look. I don't hear any sounds of life except for a faint radio at the end to my right. I follow that until I realize it's in Spanish, about the same time I discover from checking the doors with room numbers that I'm going the wrong way.

Tony Rio's room turns out to be the last door on the left, conveniently located near the fire escape. I pause in front of it and listen to Judge Wapner issuing a stern warning to someone before I start to knock.

I knock softly, but it still echoes through the hallway. No answer. After a few moments, I knock again, louder this time. Still no answer. It occurs to me that the rooms might not have private cans and Tony Rio might have slipped down the hall to take a leak. But I don't see any sign for a bathroom. I wait until the commercial breaks are over, then knock again. Same result.

Suddenly I'm feeling nervous. This isn't paranoia, it's instinct. I used to have it all the time when I worked the streets. Nowadays it only comes and goes. If you don't use it, you lose it.

I've gotten this far, I figure I ought to at least try to get a peek inside. I try the knob and push softly. The door isn't locked. On second glance, I notice that the lock is jammed. I don't know if this is standard on all rooms at the Milshire or if someone has made a special effort on this one.

As I peer cautiously around the door, I can see a pair of feet in running shoes hanging over the edge of the bed. I clear my throat loudly, but the feet don't move. I push the door open far enough so that I can see white socks and blue jeans up to above the knees. I pause to listen for the sound of deep breathing, on the off chance that Tony Rio fell asleep while waiting for me. I don't hear a damn thing. I clear my throat again, louder this time. Still no response. By this point, I'm not expecting one.

I should get the hell out of here right away, but there's something I have to find out first. I step inside and shut the door behind me.

The body of Tony Rio is slumped across the bed sideways. He's facing up, so that, with his head dangling over the side, his eyes are gaping upside down at the wall. They look to be lined up with a hole that was punched or kicked into the wall by a previous guest. At least I assume it was a previous guest.

When I get within a few feet of him, I can see whitish foam around his mouth. I also get a faint whiff of the first new odor I've encountered since the lobby. It's almost a relief from the stifling staleness. I've only smelled it once before, but I recognize it right away—the scent of almonds. The last time I smelled it, it was a suicide. This time I'll bet it wasn't.

It's hard to believe that someone I was talking to on the phone ten minutes ago could be dead already. But when it comes to poisons, they don't come any quicker than cyanide. It's a swift heart attack, triggered by immediate respiratory failure.

I have no trouble tracing the odor of the almonds to the pint of bourbon on the night table beside the bed. I have an advantage over Tony Rio. Once I saw the foam on his mouth, I knew what I was smelling for. Plus now the bottle is uncapped, and I'm not as thirsty as he probably was.

Rio's last drink was Jim Beam. My brand. The bottle is wrapped in a brown paper bag, with just the top sticking out. A note on the bag says, *WELCOME TO CHI*. Whoever wrote it didn't bother to sign it. Gosh, I wonder why.

Some people assume that if you see enough bodies in your work, you get used to death after a while. I'm sure that's true for some, but it's never been true for me. I've never gotten to know that cold blank stare well enough so that it doesn't make me shudder right down to my bones. And wonder.

Every time I see a body, it instantly triggers a flood of questions. Little questions: Who was this person? Did he have any friends? What did he have for breakfast this morning? Did he have any inkling he was going to die? And the big ones: How did any of us get here? Where do we go after we die?

Having been off the job so long, I'm badly out of practice seeing death. The last body I saw was my father-in-law's. That was over a year ago, so the questions really come flooding over me. But I manage to fend them off and concentrate on things near at hand.

Tony Rio's forehead is cold to the touch. It's not down to room temperature yet, but it's plenty cold enough to know that sticking an amyl nitrite cap under his nose wouldn't do any good at all.

That's how you treat cyanide poisoning—put a popper under the victim's nose every minute on the way to the hospital. That's a universal antidote for any poisoning. After the Tylenol killings in 1979, city ambulances all were required to carry cyanide kits. For some strange reason, a lot of the kits had to be replaced on a regular basis. Water damage was the usual excuse. The first time somebody set me up, I got accused of breaking into the cyanide kit and stealing poppers. But the charge didn't hold up. A friend of mine who's still with the department told me they cut them out at the beginning of this year. Budget cuts. They never found the Tylenol killer.

I press my fingers under Rio's chin. Rigor mortis starts at the top of a body and works its way down. It takes anywhere from two to six hours to set in. His jaw is already stiffening up. That tells me he's been dead at least two hours. It also tells me something else, the thing I had to stay and find out.

It tells me Tony Rio was already dead when we talked on the phone.

That, of course, is impossible. Which means Rio isn't the guy I talked to on the phone. Either that, or this guy ain't Rio.

I don't have time to puzzle the thing out now. Besides, either way, it still adds up to the same damn thing.

As the realization hits me, I feel my knees start to buckle. I step away from the bed, and my legs feel like they weigh two hundred pounds apiece. This is a feeling I know all too well. It's dreamlike and I think about pinching myself to make sure I'm awake. Instead I speak without thinking.

"Holy shit," I hear myself say, "I've goddamn been set up again."

6

I live in constant fear that someone will set me up again. Am I being paranoid? Sure. Do I have a reason to be? You bet.

It's a very long story. I'll try to give you the short version.

I guess it starts the night I met Frankie. That's a story in itself. I was off duty, eating dinner with a buddy of mine, Jack Egan, at a restaurant west of the Loop. It was a 911 joint, a place where the health-conscious diner smokes cigars instead of cigarettes and has the 12-ounce instead of the 16. We were on our way to a hockey game. This was back in the days when I had season tickets.

I noticed her the instant she came in and sat down, two booths away from us. She stood out a bit simply because she was an attractive woman. She stood out a bit more because she was an attractive woman in a roomful of heart attacks waiting to happen. She stood out even more because she was an attractive woman eating dinner with a guy twice her age.

He was what you'd call "distinguished," but as far as I was concerned, he was still much too old for her to be messing with. I know I shouldn't jump to conclusions, but every time I see that setup, I figure the woman's a pro. That didn't stop me from watching her. In fact, it probably made me watch her more. Because she didn't look like a pro.

We were getting up to leave when I heard the guy start to choke. Before that registered enough to make me react, I heard her scream "Albie!"

I reacted to *that* right away. I spun around in time to see Albie stand up and start to clutch at his throat with his hands. He had *The Look* on his face. I call it that because it's a universal expression people get when they can't breathe—wide-open mouth, red to purple complexion, wild bulging eyes. It gets progressively more desperate the longer it lasts. It goes in several stages, from initial discomfort to controlled panic to abject terror to absolute fear of God.

As I started to approach Albie, I figured he was on the cusp between stage two and stage three.

"Stand back." I called it out firmly but calmly. It's a tone of voice that almost everyone obeys. Even if you're not wearing a uniform.

I moved toward him deliberately, waiting for a pair of fat guys to move aside. You never want to look like you're rushing in an emergency situation. Some people can't understand that. They wonder why EMTs don't run to an accident scene. Some of them think we're lazy. They figure every second is precious and you can't afford to waste a single one. That sounds sensible, but it turns out to be penny-wise, pound-foolish. In fact, we're trained not to rush. For one thing, we don't want to make any mistakes by acting too hastily. We also don't want to create any panic. Panic is contagious. If we convey even the slightest sense of it, a whole accident scene can go up for grabs. I've seen it happen. It ain't pretty.

Albie gave me that pleading look, the one I'd seen so many times before. It's another universal expression, one that seems to say, "Please, mister, I'll give you everything I have, my house, my car, my wife, my mistress, my kids, even my golf clubs, *everything*—if you'll only let me breathe again, just one more time."

The interesting thing to me about the expression is how it differs between rich and poor. Actually, the expression itself is the same, it's the attitude it conveys that differs. And that doesn't change until after you restore their breathing.

Poor people, for the most part, thank you profusely. They're so grateful to you for saving their life that they almost do offer you everything they own. Rich people tend to be far more reserved. Their sense of happiness about being alive seems to get diluted with embarrassment for having been seen in such a vulnerable position. It's as if they'd like to slip a fifty to you and anyone who was watching if you'll all agree to pretend it never happened.

I told Albie to stay calm, he was going to be just fine. As soon as I did so, I could see the relief start to spread over his face. He trusted me. Guys in his situation always trust you when you say something like that. That's because they don't have any choice.

I moved behind him and had him lift his arms as I spread mine around him. I clasped my hands together to make a single fist, lifted them up to about the level of his shoulders, then brought them down sure and solid against his diaphragm, lifting as they made contact.

Piece of cake.

Piece of beef, actually. Medium rare, from the New York strip, senator cut. I didn't see the projectile leave Albie's mouth, because his head was blocking my view. He was an inch or two taller than me and had a few more pounds to boot. But I could feel the blockage give way at the moment of impact and hear his breathing return. Egan told me it landed three tables away in some old guy's martini.

Albie shook free from me right away, and I figured him for a guy who didn't want another guy's hands on his Armani. I figured wrong. He immediately turned, grinned, put his arms around me and smothered me in a hug so long and tight that I almost became a candidate for CPR myself. When he finally pulled back, he tattooed a kiss on each cheek, just like they do in the *Godfather* movies. In fact, for a moment I wondered if he was a godfather, but I found out he was an old-time newspaper man.

If he said thank you once, he must have said it fifty times. In the meantime, his dining companion also gave me a hug and laid a soft one right on my mouth. That was the first time Frankie kissed me.

"I tell him he shouldn't eat at places like this, but he never listens to me," she said.

Albie gave me a disheartened roll of the eyes. After what he'd been through, the last thing he needed was some *woman* telling him I told you so.

"Just be sure and take smaller bites and chew everything up before swallowing," I said.

She nodded. "I've been telling him that for years too."

That made me realize she wasn't a pro. After we did the introductions, I figured she was married to the lucky prick. I didn't find out the guy was her father until a few days later. That's when she called to thank me for saving his life. I was surprised she'd found my number because I'd only told her my name once. In the confusion, I didn't even know if she'd gotten that. I've since learned that Frankie don't miss much.

I told her it was nothing, that I did it professionally. But she offered to take me to lunch, and I took her up on it. I almost never turn down a free meal, certainly not one with a good-looking woman. At least I didn't until I married Frankie.

She'd never met a paramedic before and I'd never met a reporter. She was a second generation reporter. Her father had been one of the best in the business until he retired. Before I met them, I thought journalists were all a bunch of conniving snoops who'd stop at nothing to get a story. That turns out to be pretty much what they are. What distinguishes one from the other is what kind of story they're doing. If it has a good purpose, there's probably good reason to excuse their obnoxiousness.

At the time we met, Frankie was starting to work on a doozy. It was a big series on the Democratic Machine, how it worked, how it didn't work. Mostly she was interested in how it didn't work.

This was near the end of 1982, during Mayor Jayne's last few months in office. She had gotten into City Hall three years earlier on a fluke. There was a huge blizzard that winter, two huge blizzards as a matter of fact. They crippled the city. The streets didn't get plowed and the garbage didn't get picked up. People shot each other over parking spaces. This was totally unheard of. For years, Chicago had been known as The City That Works. That was largely a myth manufactured by the Democratic Machine. But it was a myth most people were willing to believe, as long as the city worked for them. To this day, there are still people who believe it. Most of them have held city jobs for a long time.

Mayor Jayne's election was big news, with media around the country reporting that the mighty Machine had been toppled. It was even bigger news that the person who did the toppling was a little wisp of a woman. Few took the time to look closely and notice her resemblance to the Wicked Wisp of the West.

Reports of the Machine's death were greatly exaggerated. The simple fact was that by April when election day rolled around, people were plenty pissed. So pissed that they turned out to vote in record numbers. They didn't bother listening to their precinct captains. Instead they voted Mayor Michael out of office.

During the campaign Mayor Jayne had railed about an "evil cabal" that was running the city into the ground. It took about three weeks before she started cutting deals with the top *caballeros*. Although a lot of the veteran hacks resented her, while she was in office it was Machine politics as usual.

You're probably wondering what the Machine has to do with me being paranoid about being set up. The answer is: everything. That's because the Machine has always held power over people. The Machine holds power in lots of different ways but mostly it's through jobs. The Machine gives people jobs and it also takes them away. I know all about this. I had it both ways.

I got my job through my alderman. The way I got to him was through a friend of my mother's. Mary McGuire. Her son Roddy was a precinct captain in the 41st Ward. I went to Roddy and he went to bat with the alderman for me. Two weeks later, he came back to me and said, "Come to Bingo at St. Pascal's on Friday night. Be ready to lose five hundred."

I was and I did. Roddy said I got off easy. I didn't even have to stay for the game. I just passed the envelope to a guy named Billy who was standing next to him in the hallway. Over and above that, I gave $50 to Roddy after we got outside. He didn't show any reaction. I never knew if it was too much or too little or just right.

I told this story to Frankie. I told her lots of others too. Mine was tame compared with most of them. I also put her on to some other guys. Not just guys on the fire department, but guys on the cops as well. They all had stories to tell and they all knew other guys with other stories. Before you know it, there was a whole network of guys telling their stories to Frankie. Some of them fit right into the big story she was working on.

By the way, I didn't become Frankie's whistleblower for purely selfless reasons. I had my own axe to grind. I could see I didn't stand a rat's chance of getting promoted. I wasn't kissing enough ass and when I did, it wasn't the right ass. Most of the guys that talked to her felt the same way I did. Plus I had an ulterior motive: I very much wanted Frankie to like me. And I was willing to wait until she finished her exposé to find out for sure if she did.

When the series finally ran, the Machine took it on the chops and Mayor Jayne took it on both chins. Among other things, Frankie showed how tests for police sergeant were rigged so that only guys with political clout got promoted, how the city falsified crime statistics to make it look like violent crimes and arson were decreasing, why it was almost impossible for blacks and women to get promoted. There was lots more stuff. It ran on page one for a week.

Frankie's story wouldn't have made such a big splash if there hadn't been an election coming up. It turned out to be the biggest election in the city's history. It was the election that put Mayor Harold into office, the one that really did topple the Machine. It wasn't easy, and it wasn't pretty. In fact, it was probably the ugliest campaign ever.

Before Mayor Harold, Chicago never had a black mayor. The very idea of it was unthinkable to whites, unimaginable to blacks. The only time we came close was in '76 when Mayor Dick died. The law of succession was so vague that it looked like a token black Machine alderman was in line to be interim mayor. But the city council went into emergency session and rewrote the law so that a white guy could be appointed instead.

Seven years later, the only reason Mayor Harold even had a shot to get elected was because of a personal feud inside the Machine. The son of Mayor Dick decided to challenge Mayor Jayne for the Democratic nomination. Since she had been an advisor to his father way back when, it was like a spoiled nephew going at it with his crotchety aunt. They spent much of the campaign sniping at each other, leaving Harold to talk about how corrupt the whole system they represented was. It also split the white vote.

While bashing the Machine, Harold would frequently quote from a newspaper series written by one Frankie Martin. This came as no surprise to me. Frankie's father had come out of retirement to work as Harold's advisor. As soon as he did, Frankie had to stop covering politics. She said it was a small price to pay.

The day of the primary saw the highest voter turnout in the city's history. It was especially high in black wards. Almost all the white voters in the city opted for one of the two white candidates. They split the white vote smack down the middle, leaving the black votes for Harold. As Albie had predicted on TV the night before, that was almost enough to win the nomination. But the votes that probably put him over the top were from the few white voters who crossed over racial lines.

Honkys for Harold. I was one of them.

It was Frankie who convinced me to do it. Her and what I'd seen during the campaign. Unless you lived here and experienced it for yourself, it's almost impossible to comprehend how bad the racial hostility was.

At work there was a huge rift. Black guys were for Harold, white guys were against him. You didn't dare talk about it. I made the mistake of doing so with Ron Ostrow over a beer. I'd always thought Ron was a reasonable guy. I pointed out to him that Harold seemed a lot smarter than the other two. He'd been in Washington as a congressman so he'd been dealing with major issues for years. Dick and Jayne sounded like they'd never left their neighborhood.

Ron agreed. But to him that was even more reason not to vote for Harold. "You know what they say," he said. "The only thing worse than a dumb nigger's a smart nigger."

He was dead serious. I was amazed. I'd never heard the guy talk like that before.

The more it looked like Harold had a chance to win, the more tense things got. Out on the streets, blacks I'd just helped would mouth off, telling me my white ass was out of a job as soon as Harold got in.

If you were white and wearing a Harold button in the wrong place, watch out. People would scream "Nigger lover" at you out their apartment windows. Not just men, women too. Kids who didn't look old enough to drive would yell things out their car windows. I got pounced on by two guys in a tavern where I was a something of a regular. The bartender called the cops and blamed the whole thing on me. Lucky for me, the cop who answered the call was a black guy.

I found another bar. From then on I wore that button as a badge of honor. Past primary day and right on up to the general election six weeks later. That's when things really got ugly.

For decades whoever won the Democratic primary was a shoo-in for mayor. A Republican in Chicago has about as much chance of being elected as a mass murderer.

Until Harold won the primary.

All of a sudden lifelong Democrats who'd always done exactly what their precinct captain told them to do began to take an interest in "issues." At least that's what they told the TV reporters who polled them. Democratic aldermen told their constituents to vote Republican. Brochures were printed saying Harold was a child molester. Some of the people handing them out were Democratic precinct captains.

When it was all over Harold narrowly managed to squeak into office. In his acceptance speech he declared the Machine D.O.A., and credited Frankie with putting the first nail in the coffin.

Few of Harold's opponents had listened to what he had to say during the campaign, but evidently a lot of them listened to his speech. Frankie got obscene phone calls and death threats for months. Changing phone numbers didn't help much. That made us realize she had an enemy at work, or at the phone company or on the police department. Or maybe at all three places.

Down at the fire department, I got more than my share of credit and blame. Once people found out Frankie and me were an item, it didn't take long for them to put it together that I'd been her mole. After Albie became a mayoral advisor and we tied the knot, we became graffiti regulars on bathroom walls all over the city. I tried my best to ignore it. I figured there's not much you can do for people who find it easier to hate than think. And of course it was all counterbalanced with the support of well-wishers, some of whom were nothing more than insufferable brownnosers.

Mayor Harold was the first Chicago mayor in my lifetime who wasn't known as "duh mare." After he got into office, the trains and buses still ran, the garbage still got picked up, the streets still got plowed. It was the same old city that worked. The only difference was that it seemed to work a little better and for a lot more people. Streets got paved and garbage got hauled in all fifty wards for a change instead of just the ones controlled by the Machine.

After a while it was hard to imagine what so many people had been so afraid of for so long. But the hostility remained.

It continued past Mayor Harold's reelection, when Democratic party leaders still refused to endorse him. It carried on right up until the moment he suffered the massive heart attack on that cold, dark November afternoon, the day before Thanksgiving. It even extended beyond that, though most politicians were so giddy about the opportunity presented by his unexpected departure that they suddenly couldn't find enough nice things to say about him.

For a couple of years after he died, there was a rumor circulating that Mayor Harold was wearing women's panties when he died. He wasn't. I know one of the guys who did CPR on him. But that just went to show how the hostility never subsided. All of which finally brings me to how I lost my job.

It was two years after Mayor Harold's death, right after Mayor Dickie got elected. It's not like he had anything to do with it. At least I'd like to believe he didn't. If he did, he's even more petty than I could possibly imagine. But once he was in office and the Machine was back in control, I guess a lot of guys saw it as the time to settle old scores.

My old pal Ron Ostrow turned out to be one of them. We didn't have much to do with each other since the time we'd argued about Mayor Harold. But it wasn't like we were mortal enemies. Ron knew where to get pot and he used to sell it to me and some of the other guys. Quite a few, as a matter of fact. It was no big deal, just small quantities. I'm not sure Ron even made much of a profit off it. He couldn't have.

As for me, I barely smoke the stuff. I wouldn't smoke it at all if it weren't for my wife. And I certainly wouldn't buy it if it weren't for her.

Anyway Ron told me he was planning to get some, so I put in an order for a quarter ounce for Frankie. On the day he was supposed to get it, he called in sick. But he called me and asked if I'd make the pickup for both of us.

Half an ounce of marijuana. I didn't think anything of it. I said I would.

Ron told me where to go. A graystone two-flat on Sedgwick in Old Town. Nice building, nice neighborhood. I didn't even know the guy's name. I didn't need to. Ron had already paid him. All I had to do was ring the bottom doorbell. If the guy had to go out, he'd leave it in a manila envelope inside the outside left door. That's how safe and cool it was.

The building was in my territory. I was a field supervisor, so I worked alone in a sedan instead of on the ambulance. I didn't have to answer any calls unless they were big enough to need three ambulances.

There was no answer when I rang. I looked inside the door. The envelope was there. I took it and started back down the front steps.

The cops were waiting by the car. Two plainclothes creeps. One of them I vaguely knew. I knew his first name was George, but I didn't know his last name. George gave me a wiseguy smile and asked what I had in the envelope. I gave him a look like, *You've got to be kidding.* I was sure he was.

When he repeated the question, I started to realize maybe he wasn't. That's when I *told* him he had to be kidding. Which is when his partner pulled out his service revolver and ordered me to hand it over and put my hands in the air.

I did. I was so pissed off I was shaking. I wasn't scared, just pissed. If you get caught with half an ounce of pot, you don't lose your job, you get a warning. There's a lot of bullshit you have to go through, like attending some Mickey Mouse seminar on drug abuse and undergoing urine testing. But you can get around that. If they fired every paramedic who smoked pot, there'd be an emergency medicine crisis in the city. The guys who run the department all know it.

"So Phil, tell me," George said. "What were you planning to do with all this cocaine?"

"Real fucking funny, George." I give him my best wiseguy smile.

"Funny? I don't see anything funny." He turned to his partner. "Do you see anything funny, Ed?"

Ed shook his head. "Nope. Not one bit."

George looked back into the envelope. "It looks to me like there's at least two grams here, Phil."

"Bullshit! Let me see that." I reached for the bag, but George pulled it away. I still didn't get what was going on.

Ed grabbed me by the sleeve and shoved me against the car. "Okay, spread 'em wide, Moony."

"What the fuck?" It wasn't until Ed called me by my name that I realized it was a setup.

George smiled and held up the envelope. "Gee, Phil, with all this coke here and you being so close to the school here, it looks to me like—"

"Oh shit!" I felt my knees go weak. I could barely summon the strength to glance over my shoulder at the elementary school across the street. Only a few weeks before, the legislature had passed a law making it a felony to possess drugs within five hundred yards of a school. "You assholes!"

"All of a sudden, I'm starting to see the humor in it," George said with a big smile on his face. "Aren't you, Ed?"

They hauled me in and booked me, charges on top of charges on top of charges. Most of them were dropped pretty quickly, all of them were dropped eventually. I was dropped from the fire department immediately.

It was all over the papers, front-page stories for two days running. I was identified as "son-in-law of former mayoral advisor Albie Martin" and "husband of reporter Francesca Martin." The whole thing was clearly intended to embarrass them. And it did.

I doubt the people who orchestrated it realized Albie had cancer. But even if they knew, I'm not sure that would have stopped them. Albie wouldn't talk to me at first, until Frankie told him it was her I was buying the pot for. I'm sure he was tempted to stop talking to her, but that was something he'd never be able to bring himself to do.

I never found out exactly who was behind setting me up. Ron Ostrow acted horrified when he found out. He swore he had nothing to do with it. I wasn't sure whether to believe him, so I smacked him around just in case. That got me in even more trouble. Ron said it was the first time he'd ever bought stuff from the guy. He didn't know his name, but he'd met him through Dwayne Sutcliffe.

Dwayne Sutcliffe was a field supervisor who had a black belt in karate and made sure everyone knew it. I always suspected he spent his weekends wearing a sheet over his head. I never got a chance to confront him. A few weeks after it happened, he was shot to death by a sixteen-year-old Puerto Rican kid in a traffic altercation near Humboldt Park. That made the front page too. Like me, Dwayne was on duty at the time. He got a hero's send-off, I got the bum rap. I ain't complaining. At least I'm still here.

Frankie told me there's an old newspaper maxim that her father told to her: *The next day they use it to wrap fish.* She said it's told to young reporters so they don't take themselves too seriously. She told it to me so I'd have the comfort of knowing I wouldn't be worm's meat for every radio call-in show idiot for too long.

She was right. Although it seemed like everyone knew who I was when it happened, I was old news by the time Dwayne Sutcliffe got plugged. But to this day, there are some people around who still remember it, strangers who buy me beers at a bar or stare at me long and hard in the supermarket.

I figure they must be the ones who bought a lot of fish when the stories ran. And if they remember it, you can bet the guys who were behind it still do. You never know when one of them might decide to have a little fun at my expense again. That's what worries me.

7

I was trained to stay calm during emergencies. I guess I could use a refresher course. The idea is to keep your mind and body in sync. My mind is racing to keep up with my heart. And my heart's lodged in my throat pounding double time and a half.

I take a deep breath and remind myself not to panic. Maybe I'm jumping to conclusions. Maybe it's not me who's being set up. It could be the other Phil Moony.

Either way, it's the same result. I'm sharing a room in a flea-bag hotel with a dead body. I have to split fast. Yesterday wouldn't be soon enough. But before I do, I need to take stock of things. I can't afford to overlook any details.

Like the briefcase. It's standing upright against the wall. Right under the window that faces northwest. The shade is open and I can see up Milwaukee Avenue to the rear of my building. I rush over to the window and pull down the shade. Then I kneel down and take a closer look at the briefcase.

It's a Halliburton, one of those unbreakable aluminum jobs that everybody who had anything to do with a rock band used to carry around during the eighties. They're also popular with Latin American drug dealers, at least the ones with bad accents that you see on TV.

I've got one just like it at home. I never had anything to do with a rock band or Latin American drug dealers. Frankie got it for me when we were into giving each other gifts. She thought it would be useful for carrying my medical supplies. It was, until I got fired. Now the thing sits in our basement, serving as sort of a satellite medicine cabinet until we finish the downstairs bathroom.

On closer inspection the briefcase at the Milshire has more than a passing resemblance to the one I've got at home. They both have labels pasted on them with my name and address. Of course, on this one it's actually the other Moony's name, not mine. And it's not my handwriting, like on the one in my basement. But it's definitely my address, and that's the place the cops are going to come calling when they start looking for him. I assume this is the souvenir Tony Rio mentioned on the phone.

I wonder if the person who wrote on the label is the same one who left Tony Rio the morning eye-closer with the welcome note. It looks to me like it might be, but I'm no handwriting analyst. Besides, I'm not sure I care. The only thing that matters to me right now is getting away without leaving any traces of anyone named Phil Moony.

I try to peel the label off, but all I get for the effort is gummy shit under my fingernails. If I had a pen I could try inking it out, but I don't. In the absence of cleaning solution, the only solution seems to be to take the damn thing with me. Of course I'd like to know what's inside it first.

Five to one, it's drugs. No. Make that ten to one.

I check to make sure it's locked. If it's not, I can dump out the contents and book.

Who am I kidding? Of course it's locked.

I take the briefcase by the handle and move toward the door. It's heavy, maybe twenty pounds. If it's drugs, I sure hope it's pot. Because if it's cocaine and I'm caught with it, I'll be in the deepest shit of my entire life. And I haven't exactly led a shit-free existence.

I pause at the door and assess the situation. There's a black leatherette coat on the only chair in the room. I decide to check the pockets and find out if the guy's Tony Rio.

He is. At least if you can believe the New Jersey driver's license in his wallet. It appears that Rio had a net worth of thirty-seven bucks when he died. It's a very thin wallet. No credit cards, no business cards. But there is a sales receipt from Irv's Ivy League Sports Collectibles in Princeton. It looks like Tony bought a New York Mets cap two days ago.

It crosses my mind that it might be smart to take the wallet with me. The less the cops know about him, the better off I'll be. But I tell myself that's crazy. If I take it, I'll have to dispose of it. If someone sees me, I could end up in more trouble. I decide to leave it for the cops. They can always use a little extra dough.

I also consider taking the bourbon. Chances are good that anyone who found the guy and didn't smell the cyanide would assume he had a heart attack. Chances are better that nobody will find the guy until he overstays checkout time. Unless of course someone is planning on calling it in to the cops. If someone is, they could be on their way right now, which is why I have to scram. I decide to leave the bourbon and flee.

Back at the door, I pause for one final look. Fingerprints could be an issue. I've made a point not to put my mitts on anything. But just in case, I retrace my steps and do a quick once-over with the sleeve of my coat.

I slip out to the hallway, leaving the briefcase in the doorway for a moment. I take three strides to the fire-escape door and take a peek outside. I don't see any cops. I grab the case, pull the door shut and go out the fire escape.

The stairway leads to a narrow vacant lot, maybe twenty-five feet wide. There's a two-flat across the lot, but no windows on the side that faces me. I'm only visible to people walking along the sidewalk or riding in a car coming south on Milwaukee. Even if someone does notice me, I doubt they'd think much of it. Screams and gunshots don't attract much attention in this neighborhood, unless they go on for a while.

As I step to the ground and turn, I see that I also could be visible to someone looking out the back of my office building. I plan to check the view from Artie's office when I take in his mail.

Call me paranoid, but as I walk up Milwaukee Avenue, I've got this terrible feeling someone's watching me. Instead of cutting through the alley, which runs straight west to Kedzie and which I take all the time, I walk all the way to the corner, past Ronnie's, circling back to the front entrance to my building.

I pause at the pay phone on the sidewalk outside the beeper shop. I decide I should do the right thing by Tony Rio and call the cops. Depending on how long he's paid up for, he might not be found until someone smells him. At the Milshire that could be a long time.

When you dial 911 in Chicago, your phone number and location flash on the dispatcher's screen. Maybe I should be wary about calling Rio's murder in from the phone outside my office. But I figure if it raises any suspicions, they'll be directed at the kids who deal drugs and the guy who runs the beeper shop. They could use some heat, even if it's undeserved in this case.

I make my message short and sweet, no mention of murder. Let the cops figure that out for themselves. "There's a dead man in room two-fourteen of the Milshire Hotel, on the twenty-five hundred block of Milwaukee Avenue."

As I start to hang up, I hear the dispatcher ask if the dead man needs an ambulance. I refrain from giving her a smart-ass response. She could be a trainee.

Before entering my building, I check up and down Kedzie and across to the park. It looks like a normal day. A scattering of people, mostly old folks, mostly Puerto Rican, on the sidewalk. A few mothers with babies and small kids. A few high-school kids cutting school, or maybe they're dropouts. No one is paying any attention to me that I can tell, but I still feel like I'm being watched. As soon as I get to my office, my pint of Jim Beam is coming right down off the shelf.

I take the stairs slowly, stopping now and then to make sure no one's following me. No one is. By the time I reach the third floor, I'm starting to feel foolish. But as I turn the corner for my office, I notice that the door is fully closed. That ain't right. I'll tell you why.

I've got two locks on my office door, a latch on the knob and a deadbolt latch above it that was added later. The notches in the door frame aren't lined up. If you want to lock the dead on your way out, you have to give the door a little lift as you close it. But when you shut the door from inside, the deadbolt catches about half the time.

I never bother to lock the deadbolt, because there's really nothing in my office worth stealing. The only time I do is by accident, when I pull it really hard. I could have done that on my way out to see Tony Rio, but I don't think I did.

I stop in my tracks and listen for a moment. I don't hear anything. I take a few steps closer, staying on the outside of the hallway to give myself the best angle for a look inside. I think I see something red move slightly behind the frosted glass. But to be honest, I'm shaking so much I can't tell. It could be the Webster's dictionary on my bookshelf. I've never stopped here and looked inside before.

I tiptoe two steps closer. I'm ten feet away now. I stare at the glass for half a minute. Now I'm positive I can see something. It looks like a red sleeve. Like Artie the Artist's Blackhawks jacket.

"Artie?" I call softly. But what the hell would Artie be doing in my office? And how the hell would he get in there?

I flash on Frankie's belief that Artie's a narc, the notion that I put in her head. I flash on the fact that I'm carrying a briefcase that's probably filled with drugs. If it is Artie behind the door, I'm screwed. Nonetheless, I call out his name again, louder this time. I definitely see the sleeve move.

I'm out of here, folks. I turn and head back down the long hall for the stairs. I walk softly at first, gradually picking up the pace until I hit full stride. By the time I get to the stairs, I'm sure I look like one of those ridiculous women who speed-walk with weights on their wrists over in Lincoln Park. One of the last calls I had before I got the boot was to treat a woman who managed to fracture her hip while doing that. Don't ask me how, but she did it.

As I start down the steps, I hear my office door close. I break into a run. Just before I reach the second-floor landing, I sense someone around the corner. I'm moving too fast to stop on the steps, so I jump to the landing, set my feet and pivot, poised to swing the briefcase at anyone who's there.

I'm standing face-to-face with Dr. Foots. I must look scary, because he jumps back a few steps and puts his hands up to protect his face. I give him a perfunctory nod, then continue down the stairs. When I get to the bottom, I can hear steps thundering overhead, two floors above me.

I don't wait to see who it is. As soon as I'm out on the sidewalk, I turn right and head straight for my car, zigzagging through cars driving around the traffic circle, then carving a line through the center of the square.

When I reach the monument, I allow myself a glance over my shoulder. Amidst the people on the sidewalk at the corner of my building, I can see a guy in a red jacket. In fact I can see a couple of them. One of them is getting into a red compact car parked at the curb. I don't know which one of them is the guy after me. Maybe they both are.

It might be a good idea to stop a moment and try to get a good look. But if it is drugs in the case, there's a good chance the guy has a gun. And if he wants the drugs bad enough, he might start shooting at me. I keep going all out for my car.

Fortunately, the thing starts for a change. Even though it's the law, I don't bother to fasten my seat belt. Halfway around the circle, I have a decision to make. I'd like to head north for home and have a look inside the briefcase. Instead, I cut south on Kedzie, down the center lanes of the boulevard. I want to be sure nobody's following me.

I glance toward my building as I pass it. I'm no longer seeing red. Both jacket guys are gone. So's the car that one of them was getting into.

I check my rearview mirror. There's a small red car making the loop around the square. I keep my gaze locked onto it. It turns down Kedzie, duplicating my route. It's half a block behind me. I think it's a Pontiac Sunbird, but I wouldn't swear to it.

The driver is the only person in the car. At this distance I can't see if he's wearing a red jacket. He's got on one of those dumb sports caps, like every other yuppie idiot. I can't make out the logo. These days even the symphony is selling the damn things.

I don't slow down to get a better look at him. I hang my first left, onto Albany, a short side street that curls toward the El. As I hit the curve at the middle of the block, I can see that he's about to make the same turn.

There's a chance the driver lives on this block. That's a chance I'm not going to take.

If I had to stake my life on one skill, it would be my ability to navigate the streets of Chicago efficiently. A good deal of that skill was developed driving an ambulance, which offers obvious advantages over my father's Chrysler LeBaron. But it's not all a matter of speed. I may be overreacting, but I decide to proceed as if my life is at stake.

I bolt left onto Fullerton and hang a right down the first alley. I follow that one block south. Then I snake my way east to California by way of alleys and side streets, past graffiti-scarred garages and trash-glutted Dumpsters, over gaping potholes, minced glass and wet leaves. This is the Chicago I know and love and hate. By the time I hit the 14th District cop shop at Shakespeare, I'm positive I've lost the red car or any other vehicle that may have been pursuing me.

Just for good measure, I shoot down Stave, a shabby narrow diagonal strip with a very short life span that feeds a baffling network of shabbier, narrower strips that make you feel like you're in Appalachia. From there I go east on Armitage all the way to the Kennedy.

I get off at the Pulaski exit and head straight home, right into the arms of my loving wife, not even stopping at Sullivan's for the midday pop that I could dearly use right now.

8

It's times like this that make me positive I've got a great marriage. Most guys I know, if they got into a jam like this, would go to a bar or a buddy's house to think things through. The last place they'd go is home to their wife.

I'm lucky. I can talk to Frankie. In fact, she's the only person I *want* to talk to right now.

And it's a good thing I do. Because Frankie's no slouch. She already knows something big's up. I can tell from her expression the instant I walk in the door.

"You're home early." She's standing in the hallway between the kitchen and living room with her arms behind her back. She tries to give me the poker face, but it doesn't work. If there's one thing Frankie ain't, it's a good liar.

"I'll tell you all about it in a minute," I say, holding out my hand in my official truce gesture.

"Tell me all about what?"

I put down the briefcase and head down to the basement. From the the foot of the stairs, I can see that my aluminum briefcase is still parked on the floor outside the bathroom.

When I get back up to the kitchen, Frankie hands me a glass of bourbon. "I put a little water in it. I hope you don't mind."

She always puts water in it. And she knows I do mind. But she hates for me to drink the stuff straight. She thinks that's what did in her father. I think she's wrong. I think it was the red meat.

"Thanks, you're terrific." I go to give her a first-degree kiss, but I have to settle for a peck on the cheek. Her lips are off limits right now. I can tell that by her body language. It's the same pose Mayor Byrne used to assume any time Pavarotti tried to plant a wet one on her. When Byrne was mayor, it seemed like Pavarotti was in town every weekend. She's the mayor who tried to bring high culture to the city. It didn't work.

Frankie sits down at the kitchen table with her chin cradled in her hands. I lay the whole thing out for her, every detail I can think of. She listens attentively, nodding her approval when she agrees with something I say, interrupting only to get something clarified or make an observation.

This isn't to suggest she's pleased, not by any stretch of the imagination. In fact the nods are few and far between, easily outnumbered by the scowls and headshakes. When I finally finish, she stares me down and lets out a long heavy sigh, the kind that ends only because you run out of air.

"I promised myself I wasn't going to tell you 'I told you so,' " she says softly. She shakes her head and starts rising slowly out of her chair. "But *goddamn* it, Phil! I *did* tell you!"

I could try to challenge her on this point, but I know from experience there'd be no gain in it. Although Frankie didn't specifically tell me so, she did express her doubts. And in most matters relating to decisions I make, she staked out the turf for a blanket I-told-you-so a long time ago.

"Why the hell can't you just grow up?" She's up and yelling now. Frankie has a voice that can go from 0 to 120 decibels as fast as anyone I've ever met. "Why do you insist on trying to be something you're not? When are you going to start listening to me?"

They're all valid questions. She pauses a moment to glower at me and let them sink in. She also needs to catch her breath.

The questions are purely rhetorical. I don't dare try to answer. If I did, she'd bite my pecker off. I just sit there with my head down, bracing for the second wave.

When Frankie pitches a fit at me, it always comes in waves. Generally speaking, the waves come in pairs. Each wave usually consists of three points. I like to think of them as units of rage.

Units of rage typically come in the same grammatical form—either all questions or all statements. Most of the time, the first wave is three questions and the second is three statements. Sometimes the statements in the second wave serve as answers to the questions posed in the first. This is one of those occasions.

"You refuse to grow up, that's your problem! You live in a fantasy world where everything's a game! You *never* listen to me!"

She circles the table with dizzying speed. This is vintage Hurricane Frankie. If she walked any faster, I'd run the risk of turning into butter.

"What could you *possibly* have been thinking when you agreed to meet some lowlife criminal in a flophouse? Why didn't you just hang up the phone last night like any sane person would have done? Why did you have to bring the briefcase home?

"You just don't use your head, it's as simple as that! Sometimes, I think you're absolutely crazy. And the worst thing is, you didn't even learn your lesson, you *had* to bring the briefcase home."

I only have to ride out one more pair of waves before she gets downgraded to a tropical storm. She plops back down in her chair, physically and emotionally drained. She puts her arms on the table, folds them into a pillow and lays her head down.

That's it. It's all over. That's another one of the things I like so much about Frankie. She doesn't brood about things or hold grudges. At least not against me. Once she gets something off her chest, kiss it good-bye.

I stroke her hair. "I'm sorry, Frankie. Real sorry. I really am."

That's no lie. There's nothing I'd like more than to know who the hell I am. This searching for your identity can be very exhausting. Frankie knows that. Especially since I didn't ask for a change in life. It was shoved down my throat.

"I know, I'm sorry to scream at you. It's just . . . the idea of having to go through it all again . . . it's so . . ." She starts to sob, gently. She lifts her head and looks at me, eyes damp. "Phil, I can't stand it. They're going to keep at this until they get you.

They're never going to go away. We should've moved out of this stinking town the minute Albie died."

Albie was Frankie's father. She and her brother called him that because her brother couldn't pronounce D's when he was little. His real name was Terence. How they got Albie out of that, I don't know. Even Albie didn't know by the time I met him.

"Hold on a minute," I say. "We don't know for certain that someone's setting me up. It all could be a case of mistaken identity."

"Phil, *puh-lease.* Tell me you don't really believe that. You can't possibly. Do you?"

I don't. I was just saying it to provide some comfort to her. I know how upset she gets.

She shakes her head. "I *know* it's you who's being set up. You want to know how I know?"

I nod. "Sure."

"After I spoke to you today, I decided to check the phone number that jerk gave me."

"You did?" What a good idea! Why didn't I think of that?

She nods. "I called back to tell you, but by that time you were gone. I left a message on the machine."

"So where was he calling from?"

"It certainly wasn't the Milshire Hotel."

"That doesn't surprise me. Not now that I've been there."

"Well, maybe this will. It was a pay phone. The address was twenty-five eighty-three North Kedzie."

"That's . . ." I try to visualize the location. Frankie draws me a graphic picture before I can get a fix on it.

"That's the address of your building, sweetheart."

"Holy shit, you're right." I use a post-office box for my mailing address.

"Is there a phone downstairs in that stinkhole coffee shop?"

I shake my head. "No. It's the phone booth on the sidewalk below my office."

"I should think that would answer any doubts about it just being a case of mistaken identity." She lights a cigarette and exhales heavily. It smells good. "It's one thing for someone to call your house. But to have someone calling from right outside your office, that's not a coincidence."

"I know, I know. It's not a coincidence to have someone want to meet me at the Milshire Hotel, right down the street from my office, either. But think about it. If someone was trying to set me up again, why didn't they just call the cops while I was at the hotel?"

"How do you know they didn't? You used to complain all the time about how long the cops take to respond to 911 calls."

I nod. "You've got a point there. But what about the guy waiting in my office?"

"What about him?"

"What was he doing there?"

"I don't know. Maybe it was an undercover cop, waiting to arrest you."

I think of Artie. It irritates me that I don't even know his last name. I shake my head. "Cops don't break into people's offices."

"I beg your pardon."

"I mean they don't break into someone's office to arrest them."

"Maybe he was planting some evidence." She smiles, but it's a contrived smile.

I can feel the color draining from my face. "If they check, they've already got the evidence of me calling the phone booth from my office."

"And you calling in the murder from the phone booth."

I reach over and take one of her cigarettes out of the pack.

Frankie lights it for me. "They could be planning something very elaborate for you this time."

I nod. "But like what exactly?"

"Don't ask me. You're the one that used to work with these jerks. I only know one thing."

She nods her head toward the corner of the room. At first I think she's focusing on the picture of Albie on the table. He's grinning and he's got his arm around Mayor Harold. It turns out she's looking at the floor.

"Whatever they're trying to do, I'll bet the answer's right over there in that briefcase."

9

"It's going to be drugs, I just *know* it's going to be drugs." Frankie is covering her face with her hands and peering out at me through her fingers.

I'm on my knees on the floor, working on the aluminum case with every tool in the house. This isn't really too many. If a screwdriver, hammer and pliers won't do it, I'll have to go across the alley and borrow something from Mitch Michaels. He's got a tool for every occasion. The problem with Mitch is, he'll want to come in and do the job for me. It's been less than a year since we moved into the neighborhood, and he's already fixed most of the stuff in our kitchen.

"What else could it be . . . *but* drugs?" I let out a grunt as I say this because at that moment I finally manage to pry the lid open. As soon as I do, I have the answer to my question. The contents of the suitcase aren't wrapped up in anything special. In fact, they're not wrapped at all. Not unless you call rubber bands and clear plastic sheets wrapping paper.

"Holy shit," I hear myself say. "I don't believe it."

"What is it? Cocaine or pot?"

"Neither."

"Oh no. Not heroin. It better not be heroin. Because if it's heroin, I'm . . ."

"It's not heroin, either."

"Then what is it?" She pulls away her hands and has a look for herself.

I smile and hold out a sample. "It's Mickey Mantle."

"What?"

"And Willie Mays and Hank Aaron and Ernie Banks and—"

"Hold on a second." Frankie is off her chair and down on her knees beside me. "Are you saying it's . . ." She starts to dig inside the case. "Baseball cards?"

She shakes her head as she begins flipping through them. "My brother used to collect these things. He had a shoebox full of them. But one day when he was in high school, my mother threw them all out. He was so pissed off, he didn't talk to her for a week. Neither did Albie, come to think of it. He said they were going to be worth something someday." She laughs. "Mom said when the world got to be that foolish, she didn't want to have any part in it."

"There's a lot to be said for your mother's viewpoint. But Albie was right. They're real valuable these days. At least that's what I hear."

Frankie lets out a snort. It's a nice, feminine one, but a snort nonetheless. "Just how valuable could they be?"

"Valuable enough to kill a guy apparently."

"Human life is quite a vague form of currency. And it's being steadily devaluated. Can you be more specific?"

That's my wife the novelist talking. She's gotten awfully relaxed since finding out I didn't bring a suitcaseful of cocaine home from the office. Clearly, she doesn't have any idea how much the cards are worth.

Neither do I and I tell her so.

"Come on, can't you at least give me a *ballpark* figure?" She's grinning now, the first real smile since I got home.

I stop at a card of Tom Seaver, who used to pitch for the Mets. There's a tiny red sticker in the upper right corner of its plastic protective sleeve. It's a price tag. I hold the card out for Frankie to see. "This one here's worth seven hundred dollars."

"What!" She snatches the card from my hand. I'm having a lot of trouble believing it myself.

"At least that's what the store this was stolen from was trying to sell it for."

"How do you know it was stolen?" Now it's Frankie's turn to sound stupid. I don't mind, because it gives me the chance to sound smart for a change.

I smile. "Tony Rio didn't *buy* these cards. If he did, he would have gotten a room at the Four Seasons or maybe the Drake, but definitely not the Milshire."

"You're right." She nods, then looks down at the card. "This is ridiculous. What kind of fool would pay seven hundred dollars for a baseball card?"

"A bigger fool than the guy who bought it for six."

Frankie shakes her head in disbelief. "If each of these is worth . . ." Her eyes appear to bulge as she starts to do the math.

"I don't think they're all worth seven hundred," I say.

"You're right, they couldn't possibly be."

"I'll bet some of them are worth a lot more."

"Oh, come on."

"Like this one." I hold up a card of Babe Ruth.

"Wow. Even I know about him." Her brow furrows as she leans in for a closer look at the card. "Didn't he play for the Yankees?"

"That's the reason I think it's so valuable. This is from when he was with the Boston Braves, *before* he played for the Yankees. When he was still a *pitcher*."

I followed baseball real close when I was a kid. I still follow it more or less, but the last few years it's been mostly less. It's gotten hard to work up much interest in guys who get paid three million bucks to hit .250. It's not that I resent their salaries, it's just that every time I open the paper, one or two of them are always whining about how underpaid and unappreciated they feel. Don't get me wrong, I don't like the owners, either. But with all the money they make from TV, it should cost a whole lot less for you and me to go to a game. Either that or stop complaining about how bad they have it.

I ask Frankie to count how many cards there are while I make a couple of phone calls.

"Who are you going to call—Burt?"

Burt Levison is our lawyer. He was Albie's lawyer first. He's a real good one, but he likes to play by the book. If the truth be told, I wasn't totally satisfied with the negotiations he did when I got fired. I don't mean to brag, but I don't think we made much progress until I did a private kamikaze number on one of the higher-ups. When it crossed his mind that not only could he lose his job but he also might end up sitting beside me in the slam, I think that was a breakthrough. It wasn't Burt Levison who put that thought in his head, it was me. And the idea didn't get put on the table in a conference room at City Hall. It happened in the parking lot of a White Castle on Archer Avenue.

I shake my head. "If I call Burt, he'll say to call the cops."

"Not necessarily."

"Or he'll want to call the cops for me," I say. "And then the two of us will end up going down and seeing them together."

Frankie sighs. She likes dealing with cops even less than I do, if that's possible. "I can definitely see that scenario unfolding. But that's far preferable to the cops coming to you."

"I'm not so sure they're going to come to me."

"If someone's setting you up, they'll get them here and you know it."

Now it's my turn to sigh. "I'd like to try to get a better handle on what's going on first."

"And just how do you propose to do that?"

"I'm going to start by calling Larry Little and asking if the other Phil Moony liked to collect baseball cards."

Frankie raises her eyebrows skeptically. "You're still entertaining the notion that it's all just a Hitchcock movie, aren't you?"

I shrug. "I'm holding out hope. Do you think that's really stupid?"

"Overly optimistic is more like it. I seriously doubt you're going to be able to get hold of Larry Little."

"Why's that?"

"Because I doubt he even exists."

As is so often the case, Frankie turns out to be right. I try the number Larry Little gave me and get a woman who sounds more cockeyed than he did when he called last night. She's never heard of him and she doesn't know anyone named Little or Larry, though she did once go out with a little guy named Gary, who turned out to be a very big jerk. I tell her she can't go wrong if she sticks to average-size guys named Phil.

"See, what did I tell you?" Frankie says when I hang up.

"Haven't you had enough I-told-you-so's for one day?"

Her smug look turns into a frown. "Damn. I lost count."

"It serves you right."

As Frankie starts her recount, I realize I'd dialed area code 213. That's the one Larry Little gave me, but I recall him saying he lived in Orange County. I've never been to L.A., I don't know much about it, and I'm not all that interested in knowing anything more than I already do. But I do know that 213 isn't the area code for Orange County.

I check the front of the phone book. It's 714. I dial again, using that. I get a recording that says the number has been disconnected at the customer's request and no forwarding number is available. The California voice that gives out the message doesn't sound half as nice as the one in Chicago. I'm not even sure whether it's a man or a woman.

I'm not done with the phone yet. I decide to try Dave Ginther. Dave's a paramedic field supervisor and a super guy. I'm almost positive he collects baseball cards. He collects just about everything else. With Dave it's not so much a matter of being a collector as it is being unable to throw anything away. You should see his garage. It would be the ultimate time capsule for postwar America. It's got everything from the first *Playboy* magazine and the last Edsel hubcap to bootleg Bob Dylan tapes and a Kaypro computer.

I helped Dave move once. He went from a one-car garage to a two-car. But he wasn't parking his car in it, just his junk. By the time we were done for the day, the new garage was filled up and Dave was already talking about putting an addition on it. Last I heard, he couldn't get a building permit so he was keeping his eye open for a place with a three-car. In Chicago, that's hard to come by.

Fortunately, Dave answers the phone, not his wife. I've met her a dozen times but I never remember her name.

"Phil, how are you? What've you been doing, man?"

"Same as always. Sitting around trying to figure out what color my parachute is."

Dave laughs. He's an easy laugh. "So. To what do I owe the pleasure of this call?"

Much as we'd like to stay in touch, Dave and I have pretty much fallen out of it. He's a Southwest Side guy, way down near Evergreen Park. Guys from around there tend to stay close to home. Practically the only time we do see each other is at wakes or weddings. Mostly at wakes. Not that many guys we know are getting married.

"Do you collect baseball cards?" I ask.

"I used to. Not anymore. I sold all mine two years ago. Made a bundle on them too, let me tell you. That's how I got the dough to put the addition on my garage."

"Really? I heard it was kind of sticky getting a permit and all."

"Nothing a little palm grease couldn't take care of. That came out of the card sale too."

"Sounds like you had quite a few."

"Not that many, really. You'd be surprised at how much the damn things are worth. Why do you ask? You got some?"

"A few."

"You want my advice? Hold on to them."

"Yeah, I know that. But I'm curious how much they're worth. For instance, I've got this Tom Seaver card. Someone told me it was worth five hundred bucks."

"Is it his rookie card?"

"I guess so. I'm not sure."

"What year is it?"

I check the back of the card. "Nineteen sixty-six."

"I don't remember what year Seaver came up. It may have been sixty-five. But I can tell you something. If it's his rookie card and it's in good condition, you better believe it's worth five hundred. My guess is it'd be closer to a grand."

"You're kidding."

"No I'm not. This stuff is big business, Phil, believe me. I used to have books with the prices and all. In fact, I've probably still got some out in the garage. I could check it out. . . ."

"No, don't go to a lot of trouble." If Dave goes out to his garage I won't speak to him again for a week.

"It's no trouble. I'm just trying to remember . . ." I hear him lighting a cigarette. "You know what you do? Here's what you do. There's a store on the North Side, right up in your neck of the woods, as a matter of fact. It's on Dempster in Morton Grove. It's called Home Plate."

Morton Grove is a suburb. I'd hardly call it my neck of the woods, but to Dave the North Side is all one big forest preserve, right on up to Canada.

"The guy who runs the place is an okay guy," Dave says. "You can trust him to give you a fair appraisal. You're better off going there than calling on the phone. He'll tell you how much he thinks the stuff is worth. Whatever he says, add fifty percent to it."

"That's a guy you can trust?"

Dave laughs. "Yeah, it's a crooked business, you've got to watch out. Guys will cheat you if they can get away with it. Hell, they'll cheat little kids if they can get away with it."

"And little kids will cheat each other."

"Hell, they're the worst."

"It's the American way, they get it in Little League."

"You said it. There or Boy Scouts. Anyway, I can't remember the guy's name that owns the store. For some reason, I think it might be Phil. I'm not sure I even knew his last name. I might have it in my old Rolodex out in the garage. If you want to hold on, I could try and find it."

"No, Dave, that's okay. I'll look it up."

"Well, if I come across it I'll call you." The only way that will happen is if the whole garage falls on top of him.

"That would be great," I say.

I'm tempted to invite Dave to the Blackhawks game. But I've got someone else in mind for that. Instead I listen through his update on how screwed up everything's gotten since Mayor Dickie got reelected.

Dave tells a good story, but I've lost interest in fire-department politics since I stopped working there. Maybe it's just that I can't stand not being involved in it. I'm relieved when Dave excuses himself and then gets back on to say Sherry has to use the phone. I make a mental note that his wife's name is Sherry. It's probably the tenth time I've done that, and I know full well that by the next time I talk to him I'll have forgotten it again. But for now it's firmly fixed in my mind.

Frankie looks to be working up a good sweat counting. I don't want to make her lose her place again, so I don't say anything. I just go right on to my next call.

Up until he took early retirement five years ago, Patrick Francis Ryan was hands down my favorite cop. Now he's simply one of my favorite people.

That goes double for Frankie. She'd never reveal it to anyone, but Pat was her number-one source inside the coppers for her big exposé back in '82. It took her a long time to earn his trust, but he eventually gave her lots of great stuff—in more detail than you could possibly imagine.

Unlike yours truly and most of Frankie's other confidants, Pat cooperated with her for unselfish reasons. There's nothing he hates more than a dirty cop. The only thing that comes close in his mind is a snitch. So it tore him apart to be ratting out guys he worked with. But things had gotten so bad he figured it came down to a choice between the two. He did what he thought was right. He always does.

When Pat was on the force, he held himself to exceptionally high standards. Most cops and paramedics will take a free meal anyplace they can get it. I know I sure did. A lot of them even go looking for it.

Not Pat. He wouldn't even take a free cup of coffee.

I always told him I thought that was perverse. He'd say maybe it was, but there was good reason for it.

"As soon as you accept something from someone, they think you owe them," he'd say. "And if they give you enough free coffee, after a while you start to think maybe you owe them too. So what happens when the owner of the coffee shop shoots someone? Are you going to be impartial? I rest my case." Pat always says he rests his case when he's done arguing a point.

Frankie thinks Pat is a modern-day saint. He certainly would have made a good priest. In fact he spent a year in the seminary. "I would've made it too," he once told me, "if I hadn't been cursed with such a nosy little sucker for a pecker. Check that," he said, grinning. "I mean *blessed*."

Pat and I catch up on our small talk for a few minutes before I tell him I might be in some trouble.

"I know you're in trouble," he says.

"How do you know?"

"Because the only time you call me anymore's when you're in trouble."

"That's not true." I feel myself shudder as he says it because I have been keeping some distance between us.

"So I'm exaggerating a little. An old man's allowed to do that, isn't he?"

"You're not old."

"Sixty-five next week. You don't call that young, do you?"

"It's your heart that matters."

"Yeah, well my doctor says mine ain't in such good shape. He says I've got to lay off the smokes, cut down on the booze, and cut back on my cholesterol."

"I've been telling you that for years."

"I know, I know, but when you say it, it always sounds hollow."

"Why do you say that?"

"Because every time you tell me, we're eating steak and drinking gin. And half the time you're bumming my cigarettes."

I ask if he wants go to the Stadium tonight.

"Jeez, I haven't been to a hockey game in years. Is Bobby Hull still playing for them?"

He's kidding, of course.

"Five thousand two hundred thirty-seven," Frankie says, as soon as I hang up the phone. "Of course I may be off by a few. Math was never my strong subject."

"Better count them again, just to double-check," I say.

She gets a look on her face like she wants to kill me, then goes sheepish when she realizes I'm joking. "You want to know which one's my favorite card?"

"That's easy. The one with the biggest price tag."

"No, this one." She holds it out for me to take, then watches as I look it over. "Handsome, ain't he?"

I nod. "Very." The guy's got a face that only a mother could love. And it would have to be an especially nice mother.

I flip the card over and read the stats. He was a utility infielder for the Milwaukee Braves. He played one season—1949. That was the year I was born. He appeared in nine games. He had twenty-three at-bats, four hits, one RBI, one run scored.

His name: Phil Moony.

"Have you ever heard of him before?" Frankie asks.

"No, this is the first time."

"I take it he wasn't a very good player."

"You take it exactly right."

"Well, at least he had one good thing going for him."

"His looks?"

"No, silly. His name."

I shrug. "Far as I'm concerned, the world seems a bit too crowded with guys with my name."

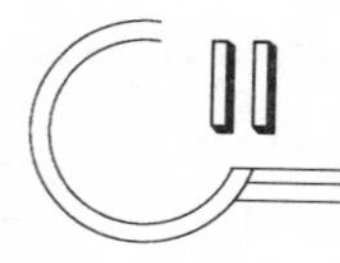

"So figuring conservatively, at an average of fifty bucks apiece, we've got . . ."

"Over a quarter million dollars' worth of baseball cards." Frankie completes my sentence for me. Math may not be her strong suit, but she's better at it than me. She also has a calculator in her hand.

"That's incredible," she says, wagging her head. "Totally incredible."

I smile. "I'll bet that's more than your brother's collection was worth."

"Yeah, a lot more. What do you think we should do?"

"I wish I had a bicycle."

"Why's that?"

"Because then I could attach the cards to the spokes with clothespins and pretend—"

"*Very* funny. I'm serious, Phil. What the hell are we supposed to do?"

"I'm sorry. My first thought is that we need to stay calm and think this through before we do anything rash."

"That's an original one. Do you have a second?"

"I think we need to find the other Phil Moony."

"And why's that?"

"Because it's obvious he's the guy the cards are intended for."

"Not necessarily. For all we know, he may not have anything to do with this."

"I'm sure he does have something to do with it. A lot."

"How do you know? It could be Larry Little just used his name to confuse you."

This is Frankie's way of figuring things out. It's a cross between the Socratic method and playing devil's advocate. If you don't watch out, it can get on your nerves real fast.

"And how did he come to pick me? Coincidence?"

"Good question. You should ask him next time you see him."

"A little while ago you said Larry Little didn't exist."

"I mean the guy who's calling himself Larry Little. Or maybe he really is Larry Little but he just gave you the wrong phone number."

"So you're saying the whole thing was made up from the very beginning?"

"Could be."

"I don't buy that."

"Why not?"

"The guy was too drunk to be putting me on."

"You mean he *sounded* drunk. It could be he's just a good actor."

"A *very* good actor."

"Or . . ."

"Or what?"

"Or maybe you're just a *very* receptive audience."

"Thanks. That's the nicest euphemism for gullible fool I've ever heard."

"Don't mention it. Remember, it was the middle of the night. You're not at your best then." She smiles and pats my hand.

I get up and pour myself another bourbon. No ice this time.

"Better watch that," Frankie says. "You need to stay sharp. Besides, it's only three o'clock."

I'm not going to argue with her now, but on a good day Albie and I used to have four or five by three. Of course if I tell her that, she'll remind me that Albie's dead.

"How do you think Tony Rio fits into this?" Frankie asks.

"Which one? The one who called or the one who's dead?"

"Both of them."

"Well, I guess the one who called is probably the one who did the killing."

"If that's the case, why didn't he take the briefcase with him?"

"I don't know. He may not have been in the room after the guy who got killed checked in."

"You mean he got there earlier?"

"Probably. Rio told me someone else booked the room for him."

"But he's not the one who ended up dead. He's the one who you said did the killing."

"Maybe I'm wrong, maybe he didn't."

"Even if he didn't, why should you believe *anything* he told you?"

"I don't know. I'm thoroughly confused."

"I suspect he's in cahoots with Larry Little."

I shake my head. "On the phone he sounded like he hated Little. And Little sounded like he was almost scared of him."

"You keep making the mistake of believing what these guys told you." She gives me a half smile. "I think Rio could also be in cahoots with the other Phil Moony."

This is when I hit exasperation point. "I thought you said he didn't have anything to do with this."

"No, I didn't. I said he doesn't *necessarily* have anything to do with this. There's a difference."

I sigh long and heavy. "Can we assume for the time being that he does?"

"Sure, why not? I think that's probably a good assumption."

"I give up. Why don't you tell me what *you* think we should do?"

She takes a deep breath. "Well, sometimes the best thing is to focus on what you know instead of getting hung up on what you don't know."

"Now *there's* an original thought."

Frankie lets out a long yawn and stretches. "You know, sweetheart, you're the one who got yourself into this mess. I could go to Mexico and not come back until you get rid of your baseball cards."

"Can I go with you?"

"No."

We bounce it back and forth like this until I'm bouncing off the walls, about half an hour. All the while, Frankie's jotting down notes on a steno pad. She holds up her hand as if to tell me to shut up, then tells me to shut up for just one more minute until she's done writing something down. When she is, she hands me a sheet of paper.

"How does this look?" she asks.

"You get an *A* for penmanship, that's for sure."

It's true, she has beautiful handwriting. Nuns would turn tricks to be able to write like Frankie. Of course it's the ideas I'm supposed to be focusing on as I look down the list she's made:

WHAT WE KNOW

Cards are stolen
Tony Rio #2 was poisoned
Larry Little may/may not exist
Tony Rio may be caller/may be dead man/may not exist
Rio #1/Little may be Artie the Artist/Narc
Other Phil Moony may/may not be involved
Man in Phil's office may be Artie (red jacket—Blackhawks?)

TO DO

PHIL:
Check up on Artie
Check office
Talk to Pat
Check on value of cards

FRANKIE:
Find out where Moony lives
Check up on Rio

I smile when I'm done looking it over. "Is this the organizational method they taught you at University of Chicago?"

"Maybe," she says coyly. "What if it is?"

"I'm glad I didn't go to college."

"You wouldn't have lasted one semester at U of C."

"That's right. And I would have been proud of it."

"Screw your pride. Why don't you tell me what's wrong with what I wrote."

"You've only got two things to do and I've got four."

"You know women can only handle half as much responsibility as men. That's why we get paid half as much as you do. Now, do you have any substantive comments?"

"It looks swell, this is exactly what I need. But I have some trouble with your fifth item. I don't think Artie could be Little or Rio. I'd recognize the voice."

"Are you sure?"

"Positive. Almost."

"What about Artie being the one in your office?"

"That could be, I guess. But if he was, then I would've recognized him. And I don't think he would have wanted that."

"Is there anything you want to add?"

I nod. "You forgot one thing on your things-to-do list."

"What's that?"

"*Nothing.* We could just sit tight and wait to hear from the people who're after the cards. They'll be calling sooner or later."

"What makes you so sure?"

"Because I'm sure they want the cards. Even if they're only worth half as much as we're guessing."

"I understand that. But what makes you think they're going to be courteous and call ahead? They could just decide to drop in."

"They've been pretty good about calling so far."

"What about the guy in your office? Are you forgetting him?"

I was. Just for an instant.

"Good point." I get up and look out the back window. I gaze through the yard and out into the alley. I half expect to see the little red Pontiac parked out there. It's not. I feel myself shudder. The idea of being holed up waiting for someone to come looking for a quarter million's worth of stolen goods is pretty scary. Real scary, the more I think about it.

I tell Frankie I'll be right back, and head down to the basement. I go to the storage cabinet in the far corner, where I keep my personal junk. When I start back up the stairs, she's waiting at the top, hands on hips.

"What's that?"

"Shotgun." I try to sound casual.

"I know what it is. What's it doing here? I thought I told you to get rid of that before we moved here."

I shrug and attempt a smile. "I don't do *everything* you tell me."

"What are you bringing it up here for?"

"I think it would be good to have handy." I pop in the shells and stand the shotgun in the narrow space between the wall and the refrigerator.

She shakes her head. "This is crazy. You're telling me you're going to shoot them if they come here?"

"If they break into our house, I will. And so should you."

"That's ridiculous. I'm not touching the damn thing."

"Then you're the one who's being ridiculous." I raise my voice, more for effect than out of anger, but I am nearing the end of my fuse. "We're dealing with bad people, Frankie. They killed one guy over these cards. They'd be willing to kill us if they thought they had to."

"Fine. Then maybe you ought to call Burt and go to the police."

"Absolutely not."

"Why not? Think about it. You haven't really done that much wrong—"

I begin counting on my fingers. "Leaving the scene of a murder and stealing evidence from a murder scene. That's enough to get locked up for, easy. I'd rather take my chances on shooting somebody breaking into my house than one of those charges. You know, Frankie, I spent a night in the County once."

"I know you did, you don't have to remind me." This is something of a sore point. The day I got busted, Frankie and Albie were unreachable. They went to the racetrack of all places, and they didn't tell me about it.

"I can tell you this right now: I ain't spending another night there if I don't have to."

"Okay, okay, I'm sorry. I won't suggest it again. But I'm not shooting that damn gun. And I want these damn cards out of the house right away, before the police come."

"Fine. Just promise me you'll use the gun if you have to."

"I'll think about it. How's that?"

"Okay. As far as hiding the cards goes, I'll do it. But right now I'm not all that worried about the cops coming."

"Maybe you should be." Frankie says this over her shoulder as she gets up and starts toward the living room.

"Who's going to tip off the cops?" I ask, following her. "Not the guys who're after the cards. I can almost guarantee it: We'll hear from them before we hear from the cops."

Frankie moves to the edge of the picture window and peers out the crack in the curtain. "Oh shit."

"What's wrong?"

"Was that a money-back guarantee you just offered?"

"Why?" I walk quickly toward her. I figure she's got to be joking. But this isn't the kind of thing Frankie would joke about.

"Because if it is, you owe me."

I join her at the window in time to see two plainclothes cops near an unmarked car at the curb. They're a perfect ethnic pair—salt and pepper, he-male and she-male. You didn't used to see that in Chicago.

"It would have been a money-back guarantee," I say. "But you weren't buying it."

"So what do we do now?"

"We get our butts into punt formation."

12

We give each other a solidarity squeeze before springing madly into action. I close the briefcase and stash it behind the lawn chairs on the back porch. We've got a screened-in porch, which makes us the envy of all our neighbors. As a result, we've also got the smallest backyard on the block.

As I head back toward the living room, I can hear Frankie letting the cops in. I hope she'll let me do most of the talking. Frankie's usually cool, calm and articulate, but when it comes to dealing with cops, she's got a real smart mouth on her shoulders.

"Area Five homicide," the guy says as he flashes his badge at Frankie.

I know him. Vic Rosten. Not well enough to dislike him a lot, but well enough to know I probably would if I knew him any better. He was working the desk in Area 2 just a few years ago, so as a homicide detective he's definitely come up in the world. But not that far. I doubt many of his colleagues would fight to be paired with a black woman. Even if she is of the young cute variety.

Her name is Shandra Washington. I don't get to see her badge, so I'm only guessing at the spelling.

Rosten has one of those square-jaw faces that looks like it's made of aluminum siding with a putty covering. He's shed twenty or thirty pounds since I last saw him. He could stand to shed that much more. That's a tough task for a cop. The temptation's too easy to do the fast-food circuit when you're driving the streets all day. Especially when every other guy with a hot dog stand is willing to feed you free of charge.

I invite them into the living room to sit down. Not out of courtesy but because my knees feel weak. When I issue the invitation, Frankie sends me a look that makes them buckle. I guess Washington sees it because she hangs back and remains standing. That leaves Rosten straddling the dividing line between the carpet and the hallway tile.

Rosten does the talking while Washington takes the notes. He gets the preliminaries about how sorry he is to bother us and how it will only take a few minutes out of the way real quick. Then he gets right to the main event.

"Mr. Moony, do you know a man by the name of Tony Rio?"

I'm ready for it, of course, but with my heart pumping it takes a lot of effort not to reveal myself. I'm not sure how well I do. Frankie will tell me later.

I count silently to three, then say, "Never heard of him. Why?" I try to sound firm and confident. That's the tone Pat Ryan advises to go for when dealing with cops. He also says you should deny everything. If you need to change your story later, you can always blame the cops for taking lousy notes.

"You sound awfully sure, Mr. Moony."

"That's because I am sure. I've never heard of the guy." I smile just a bit. "And by the way, Vic: You can call me Phil. Why do you want to know if I know Tony Rio?"

"Because he was found dead around noontime this afternoon. In the Milshire Hotel. You know where that is?"

This one I pretend to have to think about for a few moments. "Is that the one on Milwaukee near Logan Square? East side of the street?"

"Yup, that's the one."

I nod. "My office is close to there. Looks like a real nice place."

"Oh yeah, it is." Rosten smiles and the putty around his mouth gets all loose and lumpy. "I know you've got an office near there. That's why we're here."

"Why? I don't understand." They must have a lot more than proximity to show up this quick. I'm damn curious to know what it is. My guess is they got an anonymous tip, but I can't imagine why the baseball-card guys would call one in.

"What exactly do you do down at Moony Enterprises, Phil?"

I shrug. "I'm an enterprising guy. I do lots of enterprising guy things."

"What enterprises were you involved in around noontime today?"

Frankie takes the offensive and leaps to my defense. "He doesn't have to answer that! In fact he doesn't have to answer any of your goddamn questions."

Rosten puts up his hands. "All right, all right. No need to get so worked up about it." He turns his focus back on me. "You got problems with this line of questioning, Phil?"

"If you want to tell me what the hell's going on, fine. If not, then she's right. So far I've got no idea why you're here talking to me. I don't even know how the guy was killed."

He smiles, that silly putty smile. "I didn't say he was killed, Phil. I said he was found dead. You're jumping to conclusions."

"Oh come on. You're homicide, right? How the hell did he die?"

"Looks like he was poisoned. Cyanide in his Jim Beam. You a bourbon drinker?"

"Not with cyanide in it."

He chuckles. "Yeah, that would kind of sour me on the idea of sour mash."

"I'm getting king of sour on the idea of you being here." That's Frankie talking again.

Rosten ignores her. "I'll tell you why we're here, Phil. I'll give you a real good idea. We found this little slip of paper in Rio's wallet. It had your name and address on it."

"What? That's crazy!" I feel like I should get a 9.9 out of a possible 10 for that one. Probably because I am truly surprised. Along with the surprise comes a queasy feeling in my gut. I should have taken the wallet after all.

"Bullshit!" Frankie's baring her teeth. "There was no slip of paper and you know it."

"Oh, but there was," Rosten says.

"And whose handwriting was on it? *Yours?*"

He points his finger at her. "I resent that."

She points back. "I don't care what you resent." She glances at me. "It's another damn setup."

"Beg your pardon," Washington says.

"You heard me. You know exactly what I'm talking about."

Judging by the officer's puzzled expression, she doesn't. She looks to Rosten for clarification, but he's busy pulling a pack of Salems out of his pocket.

"Mind if I smoke?"

I shake my head. "No, go ahead."

"I mind." A smile spreads over Frankie's face as she lights one of her own. She would have made a great wiseguy.

Rosten looks to me to overrule her. I shrug and he slides the butts back into his pocket.

"You want to know what else was on that slip of paper?" Rosten asks. "A phone number."

He glances at Washington, and she recites the number: "Five-three-nine, three-seven-six-two."

Rosten is positively beaming. "Any idea whose number that is, Phil?"

I nod. "I've got a real good idea, Vic. It's mine."

Frankie lets out a low groan and closes her eyes. Rosten looks longingly at her cigarette before eyeing me. "You got any idea what this guy would be doing with your number?"

I shake my head. "None whatsoever." I pause for just a moment, almost perfect timing, I think. "Unless . . ."

"Unless what?"

I shrug. "There's this other guy named Phil Moony. Maybe it's him you should be talking to."

"But it's *your* phone number."

"I get calls for him every so often." I don't see any gain in mentioning that I got one last night or that it came from Larry Little.

"How convenient."

"Inconvenient, actually. Especially at times like this."

"You got any idea where he lives?"

"Suburbs, I think. A guy who called here once said he used to live on this street."

Rosten looks at Washington and watches her scribble on her little pad.

"Why don't you let us see this slip of paper you found," Frankie says.

I nod. "Yeah, I think that's a fine idea."

"I don't have it. Lab guys took it."

"How convenient." Frankie exhales hard and straight at Rosten.

"You own a red sports jacket, Phil?"

"It's closer to cranberry."

"I don't mean like a suit jacket, I'm talking about one of the ones for a sports team."

"Starter jacket," Washington says.

"Yeah, that's right, starter jacket. You own one of them?"

I shake my head. "No. Why?"

"The desk clerk, Mr. . . ."

"Sanchez," Washington says.

"Yeah, that's right, Sanchez. He said a guy came in and made the reservation for Rio a couple of days ago. He had on one of those jackets."

I think about the guy waiting in my office. I think about Artie, the artist who may be a narc. But I don't mention any of that.

"I already told you," I say. "I don't know Rio. So I sure didn't make reservations for him."

"Yeah, that's right, you did." Rosten glances around the room slowly, stopping at the photo of Albie and Mayor Harold.

"You know what else Sanchez said? He said Rio had an attaché case with him when he checked in. It was one of those aluminum jobs, the kind dope dealers carry. You know about dope dealers, don't you, Phil?"

Inside I'm seething. I now know Rosten plenty well enough to know I hate his guts. But I refuse to be riled. That's exactly what he wants.

I shrug. "I watch TV, just like you do."

"Only a lot less, I'm sure," Frankie adds.

Rosten chuckles. "Funny thing, though. When we searched Rio's room, there wasn't any case. What do you make of that?"

"I don't know what to make of it. And to be honest, I don't really care."

"I've got an idea about what to make of it," Frankie says. "I think there probably was a suitcase full of dope. And your guys stole it. They're probably out selling it right now." She nods at Washington. "In *her* neighborhood."

"You got a real attitude on you, sister," Washington says.

Frankie goes into a stare-down with her just as the phone rings. My first instinct is to let the answering machine catch it. But it's only halfway down the hall on a little table and I'm afraid it could be one of the baseball card guys. I don't want to run the risk of having Rosten overhear an incriminating message. I excuse myself and grab it.

Good thing. The voice on the other end of the line is bright and friendly, but it gives me an instant chill.

"Phil, old buddy, how ya doin'? You don't know me, but we were both born with something *very* important in common. You know what that is?"

"Yeah, I do." I turn my back on Rosten. I wonder if he can see my knees quivering. I don't say anything else.

After a long pause the voice says, "You know who this is?"

I lower my voice to a whisper. "Yeah, you're the man with my name."

He lets out a high-pitched snicker. "Or vice versa."

I don't respond at all.

"Is something the matter? I thought you'd have a lot to say to me."

"You're right. I do. You just caught me at a very bad time."

"Oh, sorry about that." He snickers again. "I didn't get you off the crapper, did I?"

If we were standing face-to-face, I'd strangle the guy, even with the cops looking on.

"No, I've got company. The Chicago police."

"Oh dear."

I imagine the color draining out of his face. But of course I can't even picture his face.

After a long pause, he says, "How did they . . ."

"I don't know." I glance over my shoulder when I hear Frankie and Washington exchange unpleasantries. Rosten is watching them with arms folded, but he looks ready to intervene.

"Jeez, you wouldn't say anything to them about . . ."

"You never know, I just might." The next best thing to strangling the guy is making him squirm a bit.

The sudden panic in his voice is palpable. "Listen, Phil, don't do anything crazy. You stand to make a lot of dough on this. A lot of dough."

"Is that so?"

"Absolutely."

"Why don't you give me your number and I'll call you back."

"Oh no, oh no. I'll call *you* back. In an hour, okay?"

I don't say anything. I just hang up. I figure that should make him squirm a lot.

As I step back down the hall, Washington is demanding to know just who the hell Frankie thinks she is.

Frankie answers in no uncertain terms and at high volume. "I'll tell you who I am, Miss *Officer*. If it wasn't for me, you wouldn't have been able to get a job on the Chicago police. You'd be dishing out the extra crispy down at Popeye's."

Even I flinch at that one. I've had my head sliced open by Frankie's tongue more than anyone, but I've never known her to resort to racism.

"You watch your mouth, bitch."

Rosten holds up his hand. "Come on, back off. It's him we're here to see, not her."

I nod. "And I think you're done seeing me."

"Sure, we're on our way." Rosten gives me a full grin. "By the way, Phil, are you still dealing drugs?"

"Fuck you."

"I take it that means yes?"

"You can take it that means it's time to get your fat ass out of here," Frankie says. She glances at Washington. "Pardon me. Fat *asses*."

They both glare at Frankie, then look at each other. "Looks like we've worn out our welcome, partner," Rosten says.

"You were never welcome to start with," Frankie says.

Rosten gives her a smile as he turns to the door. "Don't be surprised if we come back with a search warrant."

"Call first," I say. "We'll try to have some Dunkin' Donuts waiting for you."

13

My first inclination is to take a moment and congratulate ourselves on a pretty fair job of stonewalling. But Frankie won't have any of it.

She gives me the brush-off when I try to give her a hug. "I want that damn briefcase out of here this minute."

"Absolutely. And I know right where to hide it." Our next-door neighbors, the Miglins, had a fire in their garage around Christmas. They're an elderly couple who stay at a condo in Florida during the winter. Their son comes to check on the house once a week, but he hasn't bothered to go out back and check the boarded-up garage. Even if he does, I'm sure I'll be able to find a safe spot to stash the cards.

"I don't care where you hide it," Frankie says, "so long as you get it out of here."

"Of course. But I'd like to wait until it's dark."

"Fine." She looks at her watch. "It's five now. That'll be in half an hour."

Frankie almost jumps out of her shoes when the back doorbell rings. It startles me too, even though it can almost only mean one thing: Mitch Michaels, our neighbor from across the alley, is dropping by for a visit.

"Oh great," Frankie groans. "Just what I need."

I smile. "Looks like it's getting dark a little earlier than you predicted."

"Very funny. *You* answer it."

"Of course."

I head to the back porch, with Frankie at my heels. She refuses to get the door when Mitch comes over, but she likes to ride herd on me to make sure I don't let him too far inside. Ideally, she likes me to keep him on the porch. But that isn't always practical, especially in cold weather. Basically, the kitchen is as far as he's allowed to venture, unless there's a good reason to make an exception. Like when he comes over to fix something.

Mitch isn't really a bad guy. In fact I kind of like him. But once Frankie gets a bug in her pants about someone, it's hard to shake it free. She's got a big bug about Mitch, which is highly appropriate in at least one way: Mitch is in the exterminating business. And judging by the look of things—nice house, three cars, long vacation trips—he's doing pretty well at it.

One of the things Frankie can't stand about Mitch is that he smells like professional roach spray. At least she says he does. Me, I've never noticed it. She also says he always has mud on his shoes. On that count she does seem to be right. It's not the fact that he has mud that bothers her, it's that he doesn't make the effort to wipe it off. Another thing she doesn't like is that instead of making eye contact when he talks, he seems to stare at her breasts. I've never observed that and I doubt I will. I'm sure Mitch is less interested in my breasts than he is in Frankie's. I'm also sure he wouldn't try to bore holes through a woman's chest with her husband looking on.

That's what she says it feels like—having holes bored through her. I tell her I can definitely relate to the idea of being bored by Mitch, but not through the chest.

It's not any one of these things or even their sum total that turns Frankie off about Mitch. She freely admits that she's come up with these complaints in an attempt to find justification for the dislike she feels. The fact is, she regards the guy in much the same way he views the crawling creatures that pay his mortgage. "I don't know what it is," she once told me in exasperation. "The guy just bugs me."

Frankie and I have a running battle going about Mitch. I tell her I don't think she should be so hard on the guy. In addition to his home handyman skills, Mitch has another special value, and one that has become increasingly rare: For those occasions when Frankie wants to smoke pot, Mitch is the guy I get it from.

Every time we discuss him, Frankie ends up agreeing with me that she should be nicer. She even promises that she'll try to do just that. But the instant the back doorbell rings, she usually reverts to her previous perceptions.

"I'm not bugging you, am I?" Mitch asks as I open the door.

This is one of his standard greetings. It's also another one of the things that annoys Frankie about him: incessant cracks about the way he makes his living. He's got enough lines to do a stand-up routine. He told me that he even considered getting into improv about ten years ago, when it was all the rage and everyone was doing coke. He took a few classes at Second City, which is where the line ends for most would-be comedians in Chicago.

"No, of course not," I say.

Behind me, Frankie calls, "Hello, Mitch, come on in." She's really making an effort.

As Mitch steps inside, I can see he's wearing his company sweatshirt. It has a drawing of a cockroach on the front. Above the roach, in tiny letters, it says, *Don't let him . . .* Below, in large letters, it says, *BUG YOU!* He gave me one, but I haven't gotten around to wearing it. Out of the corner of my eye, I catch Frankie giving Mitch's work boots the once-over.

"Were those *cops* over here a little while ago?" he asks.

I'm not surprised Mitch saw the cops. Between him and his wife, Lydia, they don't miss out on much that happens in the neighborhood. I don't like to encourage their nosiness, so I nod but don't say anything.

"Yeah, I thought so. I saw them getting out of the car as I was coming up the street. You can spot an unmarked Chicago cop car a mile away."

"I know you can."

"I hope they weren't giving you any problems."

I shake my head. "Nothing we can't handle."

"Okay, that's good." Mitch looks at his feet for a moment, as if waiting for me to volunteer some details.

I don't.

"If you need a lawyer or something, just let me know," he says. "Because I know a couple of real pricks. That's the quality you need to look for in a lawyer, you know: degree of prickness."

"Yeah, I know. And I know quite a few lawyer pricks myself. But thanks."

"Don't mention it. That's not the reason I came over, by the way. The reason I came over is Lydia started making pot roast for dinner and she suddenly realized she has like ten times more than we need. So she says to me, 'I wonder what Phil and Frankie are doing for dinner. Why don't you run over there and see if they want to join us?' "

"That's very nice," I say. "But—"

"We'd love to, Mitch."

I turn to see Frankie standing in the doorway. I thought she had retreated into the house. She's wearing the most insincere smile I've seen since Mayor Jane's unity breakfast with Jesse Jackson ten years ago. It's the perfect smile for a bald-faced lie, which this definitely is. Frankie can't stand being with Lydia for more than five minutes. She says Lydia was born four decades too late. She would have fit perfectly into the fifties. This is no more evident than in her cooking. She uses only unnatural ingredients. If it doesn't come in a can or a jar or a pouch, Lydia wants nothing to do with it.

"But we can't." Frankie takes a step onto the porch. "Unfortunately, we've both got plans tonight. Phil's going to the hockey game and I'm meeting a friend for dinner."

She suggests waiting until the weather gets nicer and having a barbecue. That's a not-very-subtle attempt to buy a four-month reprieve, but Mitch doesn't seem to notice. Instead he focuses on hockey, reminding me that he can get tickets any time, no problem, and noting how lucky I am to be going.

"They're playing Detroit," he says. "Should be a lot of fights."

As soon as Mitch is out of the door, Frankie contorts her face into an exaggerated smile. "So: How did I do? Was I *nice* enough?"

"Yeah, too nice."

"What do you mean?"

"Nothing. It's just that you're a little transparent, that's all."

"I'm transparent? What about them—inviting us to dinner so they can pump us for info about why the cops were here?"

I nod. As so often happens, Frankie does have a good point. "Yeah, you're right."

"I always am."

"Well at least we didn't have to sit through his imitation of Arsenio," I say. Mitch has been a neighborhood legend for bad imitations ever since he did them onstage at the park talent show last fall. Johnny Carson and Ed McMahon are his specialties.

"Who's Arsenio?" Frankie asks.

"He's a late-night TV talk-show host."

She frowns, trying to place him. When her expression does not give way to any glimmer of recognition, I prompt her a bit.

"He's a black guy."

"Oh, him!" She frowns again. "But that guy doesn't have any personality. What's there to imitate?"

"That's the challenge."

I begin rising to the challenge of hiding the baseball cards by rummaging under the sink for a shopping bag. My idea is to stash the cards next door in Miglin's garage and ditch the briefcase entirely. As I transfer the cards to the bag, I ask Frankie who she's having dinner with.

"Oh, just Charlotte."

"Oh, terrific. What a time to be going out with the biggest gossip in town."

That's not just a figure of speech. Charlotte Penske is a columnist for the *Sun-Times*. She's the most widely read person in the city, except maybe for Omarr the Astrologist. The last time I got in trouble, Charlotte ran inflammatory items for a week, based mostly on scoops from Frankie. It helped our cause quite a bit in the court of public opinion. But right now, I'd prefer to keep our affairs as private as possible.

"Now, I hope you're not going to say anything to Charlotte about the cops."

"Are you kidding?" Frankie looks me straight in the eyes. "Of course not."

I take the shopping bag full of baseball cards down the back walk to the alley and slip over to the Miglins' garage. Most of the structure is boarded up, including the windows and the car door. But the side door is still hanging on its hinges. There's no padlock on it, so I have no trouble getting inside.

The place has the sooty stench of smoke that I've smelled thousands of times over the years. You never quite get used to it because it so often signifies the aftermath of lives lost. In this case the biggest casualties were a Toro snowblower and Al Miglin's collection of *National Geographics*. Despite these losses, he confided to me before they went away that the fire was pretty much a blessing. His wife had been nagging him to clean the garage for twenty-five years, and this was the only way it finally would have gotten done. He was looking forward to getting home from Florida and starting to pile junk into a new one, which he was going to have built as soon as the insurance check came through.

Without a flashlight it's difficult to see, so I leave the bag behind some charred boards in the corner, right inside the door. I doubt anyone will try to get in, but just to be safe I latch the door shut with an old padlock of my own.

Back in the house, I scrape my name off the briefcase and wipe it free of fingerprints. When Frankie's ready to go, I walk her out to her car and exact one more promise not to raise any peeps with Charlotte Penske. Before leaving, I go inside and make sure the answering machine is set. It's been almost two hours since the other Phil Moony promised to call back in one, but the phone hasn't rung. Just to make sure I didn't miss his call while we were both outside, I play back the messages. There's nothing. For some reason, the guy has decided to back off.

I pause at the back door and finally resolve the question I've been debating in my mind for the last few minutes. I go to the basement, back to my storage cabinet, and get my handgun off the top shelf. It's a two-shot .25, the same teeny-weeny model Nancy Reagan kept by her bed at the White House.

I got mine from Pat Ryan. All the Chicago cops get them. Most give them to their wives and tell them to aim straight for the heart. Pat gave his to his wife, Mary. She died twelve years ago of ovarian cancer. When I got into trouble, he passed it along to me. I never used it. But there was a time when I never left the house without it.

Those definitely were not the good old days. But in an odd way, it feels kind of good to have them back again.

There's no shortage of places where I could dump the briefcase on my way to Pat Ryan's house. He lives twenty blocks southeast in a sturdy little bungalow in Bucktown, an unassuming patch of middle-class houses that has been resettled in recent years by equity seekers from Lincoln Park. As Pat explains it, they all woke up one morning and discovered there was land on the other side of the Kennedy Expressway. At first he was amused by the parade of rehabbers in Reeboks and tickled at the notion that they were driving his property value through the clouds. But when his neighborhood saloon got sold to people who made it over with brick and ferns and started charging $2.50 for a bottle of Old Style, Pat stopped seeing the humor in all of it. Just wait until he gets his next property tax assessment.

I start out heading south on Pulaski and turn onto Avondale, a diagonal street that parallels the Northwestern train tracks and the Kennedy. This is usually a deserted stretch, but there's a car a block or so behind me. I turn east on Addison, just to make sure the car isn't following me. When I cross the Kennedy, I'm not yet sure because the car is still behind me.

I speed up and so does my heart. I take my first left, my first right, then another left. Two more quick lefts and I'm heading back down to Addison. By this time I've lost the car behind me, but I don't have the satisfaction of knowing whether or not I was being tailed.

I head west on Addison, crossing back over the Kennedy and

then turning south. I begin winding my way through alleys until I find one to my liking. Next to an overfilled Dumpster someone has left an overstuffed chair, a filthy mattress and various other home-furnishing remnants. Without coming to a full stop, I roll down the window and add the briefcase to the pile.

I go the rest of the way to Pat's on local streets. By the time I get there, I'm fifteen minutes late and he's waiting out on the porch. Pat's one of those guys who's never been late in his life. Unlike me. And he knows how to rub it in when you're late. He doesn't say anything to make you feel bad, you just do.

I apologize as soon as he climbs into the car, but it sounds hollow. As we size each other up after shaking hands, I let out a low groan. "Oh no, not you too."

"What?" He looks behind himself to see what I'm seeing. But it's on top of his head.

"The hat," I say. It's a Detroit Tigers baseball cap. I'm willing to bet he took a liking to it from watching reruns of "Magnum, P.I."

"What about it?"

"Every Lincoln Park racquetballer is wearing one these days."

"Yeah, yeah, I know. But I wear it with class. At least I try to." He shrugs. "Patrick gave it to me. I can't very well *not* wear it."

Patrick is Pat's nephew. He and Mary couldn't have kids, so he took a special interest when his youngest sister's son was born. His interest increased a couple of years later when the kid's father ran off with a twenty-year-old.

"How old's Patrick now?" I ask. "He must be fourteen or—"

"Sixteen. He's got his driver's license but no car. I'm working on getting him one so he can drive back and forth to his job. The kid's working at a goddamn McDonald's. He's saving all his money for college."

"Does he know where he wants to go?"

"Yeah, Notre Dame."

"How many billion does he have to serve in order to make the tuition?"

"How many banks does he have to rob is more like it."

"These days you'd be better off knocking over the collection basket at ten o'clock mass."

He grins as he cocks the bill of the cap. "I thought you were going to say this hat makes me look like a gangbanger."

"Oh yeah, that too. When I pulled up I almost mistook you for the leader of the Insane Unknowns."

"I know the leader of the Insane Unknowns. I played pool with him last Friday night, as a matter of fact. He's a lousy pool shooter. He's a pretty rotten human being too."

I shoot him a look to see if he's joking. He's not.

"For this community gang-watch organization," he explains. "We counsel gang kids and try to get them to start talking to each other. I told you about that, didn't I?"

He did, the last time I talked to him, a couple of months ago. And he knows it.

"That's right, how's that going?"

"Terrific. A few more weeks and there won't be any more gangs in the whole city."

"Seriously."

He shrugs. "I figure it can't be doing any damage. You should come down some night and check it out for yourself."

"Yeah, I should." The last time we talked, I said I would. "How many hours a week are you putting in?"

"A few."

"How many's that?"

"I don't know. Twenty or thirty maybe."

"But you're getting paid good money for it, right?"

"Oh yeah, I'm making out almost as good as my nephew."

Even that's exaggerating quite a bit. Pat's doing the job strictly as a volunteer. Every time I see him, I wonder just how much different things would be if he were running the police department. Not just for him or for me, but for the whole city. It's not that far-fetched a possibility. It almost happened.

In 1987, when Mayor Harold had to appoint a new commissioner, rumor had it Pat Ryan was one of the finalists. Pat was a long-shot choice since he was only an assistant commander. He was surprised, and pleasantly so, that the mayor knew who he was. He was even more surprised and pleased to find out the mayor seemed to know a lot about him.

I wasn't surprised. I had it on good authority that Pat's appointment was more than a rumor. My source was Albie Martin, my father-in-law. He was the one who'd told the mayor about Pat in the first place.

Pat didn't hear it from me, but somehow he found out he had the inside track on the job. I'm glad he didn't hear it from me. Because once he found out, it changed his whole outlook on things. Instead of being honored just to be considered, he came around to where he almost expected it. He'd never had such big ambitions before. But now all of a sudden, almost miraculously, it looked like his honesty and perseverance had paid off. In Chicago of all places. It seemed too good to be true.

It was.

Someone on the mayor's staff leaked the names of the three finalists to the press. A couple of black community groups got all worked up over the fact the mayor was even considering a white guy. Mayor Harold called Pat at home one night—I got this from Pat, not Albie—and told him who he'd decided to pick. He said he thought it would be best for the city if he chose a black.

Pat was disappointed, and not just because he didn't get the job. He was disappointed in the mayor. He thought he was above playing racial politics. Most of all he was disappointed because he said the guy who got appointed was a dirty cop. Some people would say that after decades of discrimination, it was better to have a black commissioner than a white one. Not Pat.

"A dirty cop's a dirty cop," he used to say. "What difference does it make what color dirt he is? I rest my case."

Pat took early retirement at fifty-nine. And of course he didn't retire with a small fortune the way so many cops on the take do. The whole episode left a bitter taste in his mouth. Real bitter. Five years later, and he still hasn't gotten over it. Whenever we get together, the subject always comes up. Once we're on it, we can never get off it. Especially if we're drinking. Pat put the stuff down a couple years ago, but he picked it up again after a while. You'd think his anger would have subsided by now, but if anything, he's more bitter than ever.

I hate to admit it, but it's not because I'm so busy that I don't call Pat much anymore. It's his bitterness that does it. It seems like every time I see him, I come home depressed. I don't need that. Neither does Frankie. But it bothers me that I feel that way because I know Pat could use a friend.

"So, tell me about your troubles," he says as I turn down Ashland Avenue.

"It's too long a story to tell you before the game starts."

"So give me the short version. Twenty-five words or less."

I take a deep breath. "I ended up in a hotel room with a dead body around noon today. By three o'clock the cops came to my house asking about the guy."

"What hotel, what cops?" There's no trace of shock in his voice. You can't shock the guy.

I tell him.

"One fleabag and at least one scumbag. I don't know any Shandra Washington. Tell me more."

I get as far as getting the briefcase home when we reach the line of cars on Washington Street on their way to the game.

"So I finally get the damn thing pried open. And guess what's in there."

"That's easy. Drugs."

"Wrong."

"Money."

"Wrong again."

"Guns."

"Three strikes and you're out. *Baseball cards.*"

"Baseball cards! That's ridicu—" Pat pulls off his cap and scratches at his hairline. "You know, those suckers are supposed to be worth a lot of money these days."

I nod. "I figure these are worth two hundred K."

"Nah, come on."

"Easy." I tell him about Frankie's count and the price tags on some of them.

"Son of a bitch. Patrick had a pretty good collection. Until Colleen got the bright idea to throw them out. He didn't talk to her for a week. Neither did I when I found out about it. She didn't throw them away, actually. She donated them to Goodwill. So you know where they went, don't you?" He waits a moment for me to look at him. "Right to the director's kid."

"You never know. The director may have kept them for himself. I'm going to take some of them to a store tomorrow, get an appraisal."

"Be damn careful doing it. And the first thing you should do is stash the cards someplace nobody can find them."

"I already took care of that. They're in my next-door neighbor's burned-out garage. He's in Florida for the winter."

"That's good. That means you can get to them quickly if you need to. Have you heard from them yet?"

I tell him about the call from the other Phil Moony and my concern that he didn't call back.

"I wouldn't worry about that. He will. What I would worry about, if I were you, is your wife. You didn't leave her home alone, did you?"

"She's out to dinner."

"Well, you should make a point of getting back there before she does. These don't sound like the kind of guys who shoot guns, but you never know what they'll do."

We pull into the lot on the north side of Chicago Stadium. Across the street is a line of high-rises, decaying redbrick plastered with graffiti, windows broken, garbage strewn in front. These are the Henry Horner Homes, one of the city's many ill-devised public housing projects.

Pat shakes his head as he surveys the squalor. "You'd think the guy would throw a few bucks across the street to clean it up a little bit, wouldn't you?"

"Not this guy, you know that."

The guy is Bill Wirtz, owner of the Blackhawks, the Stadium, and half the real estate on the West Side.

Pat yawns and stretches as he gets out and surveys the Stadium. "It must be a tough life inheriting a ton of money."

"Two tons is what I hear."

"I haven't been inside this place since the son of a bitch let Bobby Hull leave town. That was twenty years ago. I'll bet it's a lot different."

"This may come as a shock to you, Pat, but the goalies wear masks to protect their faces these days."

"You're kidding!" His surprise is affected, but when he takes his ticket from me and looks it over, he suddenly sounds authentically startled. "You're *kidding*."

"What's that?"

He waves the ticket. "Did you pay thirty bucks for this?"

"Sure, don't worry about it."

"I don't want to see a game that bad."

"Are you serious?"

"Damn right I'm serious. I'm more interested in hearing about your situation over a beer than seeing a hockey game. Can we sell these things? You can buy a lot of beers for thirty bucks."

"Are you sure?"

"Sure I'm sure. I haven't been to a game in twenty years, what's one more day?"

It takes me all of five minutes to find a couple of suits in town on business from Detroit. I could stick them for $50 apiece easy, but with Pat looking on I feel compelled to do the ethical thing.

Pat laughs as we start back to the parking lot. "This way we beat the traffic leaving the game."

As I glance over my shoulder, I catch sight of a familiar figure bounding along the sidewalk near the main entrance to the Stadium. He's got his arm around a woman with long blonde hair spilling over a black fur coat. As soon as I see him, I wheel all the way around to make sure I'm not mistaken. I could be. After all, there are a lot of big guys with blond hair who wear Blackhawks jackets. Especially at Blackhawks games.

They're about fifty yards away. I yell out his name as loud as I can. I'm not sure it's loud enough to penetrate the din. He doesn't respond at all.

Pat turns around. "What's going on?"

"I'll be right back."

I take off at a half-sprint, angling my way through the crawl of cars on Warren Street. Ahead I can see the couple entering the main gate, maybe thirty yards away. Inside, there's another set of doors where the ticket takers are stationed. I won't get through there without a ticket.

I sidestep my way past clusters of people. When I reach the gate, I manage to catch sight of them being sucked through the turnstiles. I shout out his name again. This time he pauses, as if he's dimly aware of someone calling him. But he continues on, and my next attempt falls on deaf ears.

"What was that all about?" Pat asks when I join him back in the lot.

"That was Artie, the guy who gave me the hockey tickets."

"Are you sure?"

"Almost positive."

"He's back from New York a little soon, wouldn't you say?"

I nod. "It's as if he never left."

15

"This isn't a cop job," Pat says. "At least not just to nail you. If it was, they would've been waiting outside the hotel."

We're at a tavern near Pat's called Rick's First One Today. I like the name, but I'm afraid, judging by how friendly Pat is with Rick, that he's been having his first one pretty damn early most days.

"If cops are involved, I'd say it's just one or two of them using you as a courier to pick up the cards," he says.

"But why? Why wouldn't they just do it themselves? One of them already went there and made a reservation for the guy."

"It's stolen stuff. Let's say someone is following this guy Rio. Maybe the cops, or maybe the guys he stole the stuff from. They probably didn't want to risk that. That makes sense, doesn't it?"

"I suppose. But it still seems like they went to a lot of trouble."

"Trouble for who? Not for them. For you."

"Yeah, but I've got the cards they want."

"Don't worry, they'll come get their cards."

"That's what does make me worry."

"Sure, of course it does."

"So you don't think I should get my lawyer and talk to the cops?"

Pat scowls and shakes his head. "You can talk to your lawyer all you want, but why would you even think about going to the cops?"

"That's what my lawyer would probably tell me to do."

"Then stay away from the lawyer. Or get another one."

I'm glad to hear him say this. Despite my insistence to Frankie, I've been wondering if I shouldn't come clean.

"So you don't see any reason to talk to the cops?"

"None whatsoever."

"Not even for moral reasons?"

"Moral reasons! Ha!" He washes down the rest of his beer and beckons Rick for another. This will be his third and we've only been here fifteen minutes. "You didn't do anything wrong, Phil. You did something stupid, but it wasn't wrong. If you're worried about morality, go talk to a priest. But don't go to a cop."

As Rick approaches with a beer, Pat lowers his voice. "You go to the cops on this, Phil, and you're going to have nothing but trouble on your hands. So they don't have enough to convict you, right? But that doesn't mean they won't keep hounding you or that they won't arrest you. These guys will make your life miserable if they can. And they'll enjoy doing it.

"Right now, they've got nothing on you. Even when they find out the call about the stiff was made from the phone outside your building, they've still got nothing. And they will put that together, if they've got any brains at all. Which, by the way, is never a given.

"Now you're sure you wiped the room clean of prints?"

"Positive."

"Fine. Then they've got nothing. No matter how much they press you, deny it. Understand?"

I nod, and I can see that Rick is taking it as a request for another beer. There are only two other guys in the joint, and he seems to be naturally quick on the draw.

"The question I need to figure out is why they picked me."

Pat shakes his head. "The question you need to figure out is who picked you. Once you know that, you can decide how to deal with them. That's when the moral questions arise: Do you hand over the cards and have yourself a nice little payday? Or do you put the cops on to them?"

I start to answer but he waves me off. "There'll be plenty of time to decide. For now we should focus on the little questions. Like how do you think this guy got into your office?"

"I don't know. I didn't have a chance to check. I assume he just picked the lock."

"That's not a skill many people have. Anyone you can think of who has a key?"

"My landlord."

"Anyone who might have access to your keys, someone you loaned them to once."

"Well, Frankie's got a set, of course. And . . ." I pause for a moment. "And you, now that I think of it. Remember when we went to Mexico and you house-sat?"

"I don't count. I don't need a key. I know how to pick a lock." Pat grins as he finishes off another beer and lights a cigarette. I give in and have one too.

"By the way," he says, "do you keep a set of keys in your office?"

"Yeah, in my desk."

"What all's on it?"

I take a sip of beer. "The office, my car, oh shit!"

"Your house keys?"

"Yeah." I start to get up.

"Where you going?"

"I better go home, make sure no one's broken in."

"Not so fast. You'd be better off checking your office, see if someone took the keys. That way you can also check up on Artie, maybe find out what his last name is. If I have that, I can find out if he's a narc."

"Okay, let's go." Suddenly, I'm feeling claustrophobic. I don't want to hang around the bar drinking all night.

"I'll be back," Pat promises as we wander out. When we get into the car, he starts to recite a list of what has to be done.

"We need to check your office. We need to find Moony. We need to find out more about Rio. We should also check on this guy Little. What was the name of this club he said he owned?"

"Do you think it could be real? Frankie's got me thinking he made the whole thing up."

"Maybe he did. There's one way to find out."

"Okay. It was called Purple Haze."

"Rush and Walton?"

"Around there. Why? Do you know it?"

"Yeah, I think I remember the place. A little shithole. One of forty gazillion names they've had for that place, if I'm thinking of the right spot."

He shakes his head and laughs. "When I was a patrolman, I used to spend half my life going up and down that Rush Street strip. And it wasn't even my district. The guy who broke me in, an old guy, Mulrooney, it was his idea. There was this pair of vice cops who were on the take and he knew about it, he had their whole act figured out. He knew what day they did their rounds. So on that day, I think it was every Tuesday, we'd follow them around, just in case they had a car accident. If they did, I was supposed to run up there and grab the bag of dough."

"You're kidding."

"I wish I was. They never had an accident. But one day, *we* did. Because this asshole ran a goddamn red light trying to keep up with them. And then the son of a bitch wants me to say I was driving."

"How long were you partners?"

"Too long."

"Seriously."

"Three, four months maybe. He dropped me as quick as he could."

As I park on Kedzie right below my office, I realize I've never been inside the building at night. I have to use my building key to open the inner door. During the day that door usually stands open. The stairway is dark. Not so dark that I have to turn on my flashlight, but dark enough to give the whole place a spooky feeling. The steps seem to creak more than usual and the sound echoes through the building.

We head for my office first. I hold the flashlight while Pat checks the lock. He doesn't think it's been tampered with.

"Artie," I say. "I'll bet he grabbed the key when he came into my office this morning." It's hard to believe that was just this morning. It feels like a week ago.

Inside everything seems to be in order, which means the place looks just like the sloppy mess it usually is.

"I know a retired lab guy," Pat says. "Maybe I can get him in here tomorrow to dust the place for prints."

"That sounds like a fine idea. What do you check them against?"

He nods. "That'll be a little trickier."

I slide open the top right drawer first. That's where I keep my keys. "They're right here," I say as I slip my hand under the yellow legal pad that covers them.

"That means nobody took them. Or somebody did take them and had the balls to come put them back."

"Which do you think?"

"Probably the first. The reason you'd return them is so someone wouldn't know they were missing in the first place. But the guy who was in here knows you saw him, so he'd be better off keeping them. If he was smart. They're not always."

"Well, I don't see anything out of place."

"Take your time and take a good look," Pat says. "It's not as easy as you think to notice something that's not there."

I don't notice anything at first. Until I offer him a drink.

"What do you have?"

"Gin, bourbon, scotch." I look to the end of the bookshelf, the spot I call my Executive Lounge. "Correct that, nothing." I get up and walk over there. "There's no booze. Someone took it."

"How much was there?"

"I had a fifth of Beefeater, a pint of Johnny Walker and . . ." All of a sudden my stomach feels very queasy. "And a pint of Jim Beam."

"That's what the cyanide was in, wasn't it?"

"Yeah, that's right." I have to sit down in my chair.

"And Vic Rosten made a point of mentioning it?"

"He mentioned it. I don't know if he made a point of it."

"Shit." Pat puffs up his cheeks and blows out hard. "I may be wrong about them not trying to set you up, pal."

"I know, you don't have to tell me."

"How long have you had it?"

"I just bought it a couple of days ago."

"Was it here when you left for the hotel?"

"I don't remember."

"Try."

After twenty seconds I let out a long breath. "I can't."

"Okay." Pat steps over to me and puts his hands on my shoulders. He stares me down with his bloodshot eyes. "If your prints turn up on the bottle—"

I force a smile and finish his sentence for him. "That's when I call my attorney."

"Yeah, because you'll be in deep shit. But I'm getting you the fuck out of it, *promise.*"

"Thanks a lot."

"Until then, far as you're concerned, some fuckhead stole your booze. It won't help anything to worry about it, right?"

"Right."

"Okay, so let's go check out this scumbag Artie's office."

When we get to the other side of the building, I'm certain Artie would have a perfect view of the Milshire from his window. Pat holds the flashlight while I slide the key into the lock. It fits, but that's all it does. No matter how much I jiggle it, it won't turn the tumbler.

Pat gives it a try. "Son of a bitch." It won't work for him either.

"Are you going to pick it?"

He shakes his head. "I'm afraid I'd need some tools with one of these."

I hold up the key that Artie gave me. "I wonder what this goes to." I can tell from the shape and the logo that it was made at the

Ace Hardware on Fullerton, the same place the key to my office and the key to the building were made. "Maybe Artie gave me a copy of the building key by mistake," I say, holding those keys parallel and comparing them.

"By mistake?"

"I'm giving him the benefit of the doubt."

"You're a thoughtful guy."

It doesn't fit. I hold it up against the key to my office. "I don't fucking believe it."

"Better try it, just to make sure."

"Now who's giving the guy the benefit of the doubt?"

We walk quickly to the point of the building and I put the key into my lock.

"Son of a bitch," Pat says as the door opens.

"But that doesn't make any sense," I say. "Why the hell would he give me my key?"

"I don't know, it sure doesn't. Unless the guy's really trying to fuck with your head. You sure you've never met him before?"

"Positive. Never."

"Well, we better find out the son of a bitch's name. I need to check this guy out."

"I can call my landlord and ask him. I'll do it right now, as a matter of fact."

I flip through my Rolodex until I get to Jerry Gabriel. He lives in the suburbs, like so many of the people who own property in Chicago. I don't have his address, just his phone number. Jerry prefers to collect the rent in person. I've never asked why. I assume he doesn't want his tenants to know where he lives. Either that, or he doesn't want his wife to know how much dough he's making. I don't even know if Jerry has a wife.

I get an answering machine. The voice doesn't sound like Jerry's, but that could be an illusion. In person it's hard to isolate Jerry's voice from the gold chains and turtlenecks he wears. The message identifies itself only by number. I check to make sure it's the same one I've got in my Rolodex. It is.

At the beep, I tell Jerry I'd like to get Artie's name and

number. I say I had it written down but lost it. I give him two numbers, home and office, and tell him to leave the information on my machine if I'm not in. I refrain from saying it's important. I don't want to arouse any suspicion or even any interest on his part. As landlords go, Jerry's okay. But he's no angel by any means. I've got good instincts about some things, and something tells me Jerry's putting a lot of white powder up his nose.

I decide I should head home before Frankie gets there. Pat offers to accompany me. When I try to discourage that notion he insists on it. I realize this is the most valuable he's felt in a long time. To save me the trouble of driving him home later, we swing by his place to get his car. He directs me to the alley behind his house.

"You like my new car?" he calls as he opens the garage door.

I have to get out and come around my car to get a good look. When I get close, I do a double take. It's a Pontiac, red and small.

"Sunbird?" I ask.

"No. They call it the Fiero. It's the kind Patrick wanted me to buy." Pat grins. "It's the first brand-new car I've ever owned."

"It's about time." I don't say anything to him, but now I know what kind of car was following me earlier today.

"Yeah, you said it." He opens the passenger door and reaches into the glove compartment. When he pulls himself out, he beckons me over. He holds out his right hand. I reach out and feel the chill of steel.

"I want you to take this. It's only got two shots, so aim good."

I shake my head. "You already gave me one. Three years ago. I've got it in my glove box."

"Then give this one to Frankie."

"She won't have anything to do with the damn things."

He takes the gun back. "We'll see about that, after I chat with her."

"That's a chat I'd really like to see."

I feel like we're on a TV cop show, Pat and me, as we tiptoe up my back steps, each holding a gun. To anyone watching, it would probably look like one of those comedy cop shows, because Pat's gun is about four times the size of mine.

I slide the key gently into the lock, push open the door as far as it will go without creaking, and ease through the opening onto the porch. I pause there for half a minute. Not a sound.

Pat nods for me to continue on in. I go as far as the kitchen, where the overhead light is on from when I went out. I check for signs of an intruder. Nothing.

From there we move to the dining room. Everything looks to be in order there too, until I see the envelope.

It's regular size, number 10 I think it is, and my name is printed on it. As I reach for it, Pat waves me off. He picks it up by the corner with the thumb and index finger of his left hand and stands it on end. With the edges of the envelope balancing against his fingers, he slices it open at the top end, using the utility knife he keeps on his key chain.

"Fingerprints, maybe," he says softly. It's the first word spoken between us since we entered the house. He guides a sheet of paper out gingerly, fingers only touching the folds of the paper.

Pat uses his palms to unfold the letter. It's not much of a letter, just a few words. That becomes clear when he lifts it and the $500 bill flutters out.

Dear Phil—Thanks a mil
Your pal—Larry Little

"So much for Frankie's notion that Larry Little doesn't exist," I say.

"I'm sure she'll be real impressed to find out he's a pal of yours. Five hundred bucks. Seems like a very generous guy."

"My friendship doesn't come that cheap."

"Yeah, that's what I used to tell people. You want to even *think* about buying me off, pal, the opening bid's a grand." He laughs. "Son of a bitch if some of them wouldn't hand it over without even blinking."

"What would you do then?"

"I'd tell them no amount of money from a scumbag like them would do. Man, that would really piss some of them off." Pat lights a cigarette. "Anyway, it looks like your pal Larry must've got what he was after."

"That's impossible." I turn and head for the back door.

"Where you going?"

"Next door to check on those cards."

"You got a flashlight?"

"Good point." I head down to the basement to get one while Pat waits at the top of the stairs. When I get back up there, I've got the flashlight in my hand and a 500-watt grin on my face.

"What are you so happy about all of a sudden?"

"I think I know why Larry Little left the note and the money."

"Why?"

I tell Pat about the temporary bathroom cabinet that's stored in my aluminum briefcase. "It's gone. He probably thought I stashed it downstairs."

"I'd check the garage just to be sure."

We do. The cards are still there. Since I have the flashlight with me, I take the time to hide the bag behind a stack of boards so that you can't see it unless you're looking for it.

"That's rich." Pat lets out a laugh. "I'd like to see the guy's face when he opens the case expecting to find Mickey Mantle and finds toothpaste and deodorant instead."

"I'd just like to see the guy's face, find out what the hell he looks like, who the hell he is."

"I expect you'll have your chance."

When we get back inside, Pat looks for signs of forced entry while I work on finding us some bourbon. My efforts are more successful.

"Nothing that I can see," he says as he takes the glass from my hand.

"So this means someone got in here with a key."

"Afraid so." We toast, and his gaze goes to the refrigerator, where Frankie has affixed the Phil Moony baseball card with a Sears Tower magnet. "I didn't know you played in the Bigs."

"Neither did I, until this afternoon. And that guy barely did either."

He pulls the card down, turns it over and inspects it. "How much do you suppose it's worth?"

"I don't know. There's no price tag."

He grins. "I guess that makes it priceless, right?"

"To the right fool, everything is priceless."

"You're sounding awfully philosophical all of a sudden."

"I'm quoting my dead father-in-law."

Pat holds out his glass. "Wasn't he also the guy who said, 'Why settle for one drink when you can have two?' "

I nod. "One of the guys who said it, I'm sure."

"So, do you know a good locksmith?"

"Not offhand."

"Well I do. You want me to call him for you? It might help with the price."

"If you don't mind."

"Don't mind at all, you know that."

"Do you think I should have him out here tonight?"

"I would. No sense taking any chances. I suspect your pal Little will phone first and try to arrange a deal. But you never know. He could just decide to come back."

While Pat's using the kitchen phone, I go to the hallway and play back my messages. There's no word from Phil Moony, but three times someone has called and hung up without leaving a message. As I rewind the tape, I hear someone on the front steps.

Pat hears it too. He appears behind me, poised with his gun. I make a quick dash across to the living-room window and peer out the curtains.

"It's Frankie," I tell him.

We try to act normal, but it's too late. As Frankie swings the door open, she's treated to the sight of me backpedaling down the hall with Pat lurking behind me.

"What's going on?" Her greeting seems entirely appropriate under the circumstances, but I try to buy a reprieve.

"Aren't you going to ask how the hockey game was?"

"No, I'm not. What's going on?"

Pat and I exchange sheepish glances. Frankie strides right up to him and gives him a hug. "It's so nice to see you again, Pat." Then she turns to me. "Well?"

"When you came to the door we were afraid someone was breaking in," I say.

"Didn't you hear me turning the key?"

"Yeah, we did. But we thought the person breaking in would have a key too."

"What? Why do you think that?"

"Because somebody's already been in the house tonight. And they had a key."

"What!" She lets go of her purse and it hits the floor with a thud.

I give her a brief summary of the evening's events, watching her eyes widen and her jaw drop until she sags into a dining-room chair and covers her head with both hands. I spare her the part about the bourbon missing from my office. I'm not sure she'd be able to handle that. Or that I'd be able to handle her reaction. When I finish, she gradually raises her head and peers out at me through a forest of hair.

"So, if we had just left the cards out on the table, this whole thing would've been over now."

I nod. "Maybe."

"But I made you get them out of here."

This is classic guilt-seeking behavior. I figure Frankie had a few pops with Charlotte Penske. In addition to being our town's biggest gossip, Charlotte is one of our most prominent lushes.

"Don't start blaming yourself," I say, though I must admit I don't mind having some of the heat taken off me.

"Yeah, you made the right move getting the stuff out of here," Pat says. "There's no way you could've known."

"So now what the hell do we do?" she asks.

"To start with, we're changing all the locks. Pat called a locksmith. He's on his way."

"And, if I can make a suggestion," he says, "I don't think you guys should sleep here tonight. You can stay at my place."

"Oh no, absolutely not." Frankie is up and standing again. In fact she's moving toward the liquor cabinet. "It's not that I don't appreciate your offer, Pat, I just refuse to be driven out of my own house."

I can generally tell from Frankie's tone when she's willing to bend. This is one of those occasions on which I'm certain she's an immovable object. If the alternative wasn't staying at Pat's, I still might challenge her. He's got three cats and only vacuums once a year. But he'd be insulted if I brought up the idea of going to a hotel.

"Okay, I understand exactly where you're coming from," Pat says to Frankie. "But in that case, I want to have a word with you." He turns to me. "Do you mind if I talk to your wife alone for five minutes?"

I give them ten while I make a pot of coffee. That's what we need. When I return to the dining room, Frankie is holding the little .25 in her right hand. "Annie Oakley," she says, smiling at me.

I pull mine out of my jacket pocket. "Bond, James Bond."

* * *

Pat hangs around for another hour or so, until the locksmith is done. Even including Pat's built-in discount, the guy makes a small killing. By now it's pushing two o'clock. Having new deadbolts on the doors lets us breathe a little easier, but it doesn't enable me to sleep any better.

I spend most of the night camped out in a chair in the bedroom with the shotgun by my side. A few minutes after four, the phone rings. I figure it's got to be Larry Little, but I'm wrong. Whoever it is stays on the line half a minute and treats me to a little hyperventilation lullaby before hanging up. He doesn't call back. The next thing I know I'm lying in bed and Frankie is standing over me, shaking me awake.

She's got a cup of coffee in one hand and the *Sun-Times* in the other. She waits for me to steady myself, then gives me the coffee. As soon as I've had a sip, she drops the paper on my lap. It's open to the obituary page. Then she drops the bomb.

"I think there's a real good reason why Phil Moony didn't call you back."

"What!" I lean in to read, and spill half of my coffee.

The obituary is only two paragraphs, not as long as you'd expect for a guy who played nine games in the major leagues. According to the obit, Moony also was an avid collector of baseball memorabilia. He died of a heart attack two days ago. He was sixty-two. He lived in Winnetka but was born in New Jersey and grew up in Milwaukee. Survivors include his wife, Elizabeth (Betty), a former runner-up in the Miss Wisconsin pageant; a son, Jason; and a daughter, also named Elizabeth.

"What do you think of that?" Frankie asks as I take a sip of coffee, a signal that I'm done reading.

"This is weird. This is just too damn weird." I wave the paper. "This says he died the day before yesterday. Which explains why he didn't call back. But it doesn't explain how he was able to call me in the first place. Who the hell's doing this?"

Frankie shakes her head. "You're starting to make a habit out of talking to guys on the phone after they're dead, Phil."

I'm trying extra hard to stay calm. "Just Rio and Moony.

Two's not that many when you consider I've been alive forty-three years."

"Lately it's been happening at the rate of twice a day."

"I doubt it can keep up at this pace for too long."

"The funeral mass is private, but there's a wake tonight. Do you think we should go?"

"Definitely."

"Do you think it's just a coincidence that he died now?"

"Definitely not."

17

"Good morning, Mr. Sanchez, this is Detective Rosten with the Chicago police." I'm standing at the kitchen counter, flipping backwards through the *Sun-Times*. I drop my voice an octave in an effort to sound dumb, but it's hard to duplicate Rosten's moronic tone. Besides, I'm pretty sure the effort is lost on the desk clerk at the Milshire Hotel. Frankie made a note of his name when Rosten mentioned it yesterday.

"Mr. Sanchez, I'm just checking to see if you can recall or if any of your tenants recall seeing anyone in the hotel yesterday that looked out of place?"

"No, like I told you, I didn't see nobody."

"Yes, I know, but you're sure none of the other people at the hotel told you about seeing anyone who didn't belong there?"

"I don't know, you'd have to ask them."

"Mr. Sanchez, you told us the man who reserved the room for Tony Rio was wearing a red sports jacket. Can you remember if that was a Blackhawks jacket or a Bulls jacket?"

"I don't know, man. I told you. It was red and shit."

"Yes I know. But did it have an Indian head, like the Blackhawks? Or was it the head of a bull, like on a Bulls jacket?"

"Hawks, Bulls, what's the difference? The people who wear them are all scumbags, you know what I mean?"

"Mr. Sanchez, can you tell the difference between a taco and a tostada?"

"Sure. What's that got to do with it?"

"Then you should be able to tell the difference between a Hawks jacket and a Bulls jacket."

"Well I can't, okay, man? Is there a crime against that?"

"No, there's not. Thank you, Mr. Sanchez, you've been lots of help."

He has, in a way. He's provided me with some relief about the chance I might have been seen. That looks highly unlikely. I was also hoping to narrow down the possibility that it was Artie who made the room reservation. Even though Sanchez couldn't help with that, I find comfort in his vagueness. I'm sure Rosten will have occasion to call him later today. When he does, I'll bet Sanchez will be feeling even less cooperative.

I go back and read the Phil Moony obit one more time while I dial up my landlord, Jerry Gabriel. I don't see anything new in it that I didn't notice before.

It's before nine, and I have a feeling Jerry had a late one last night. He doesn't answer until the fifth ring.

"You sound like I feel," I say.

"If you feel like I feel, you shouldn't be calling so early."

"Sorry. Did you get my message?"

"Yeah, I got your message. I was at a wake. And no, I don't have his number. He told me he was changing it and he'd give me the new one when he got it, but he never did. I got his address, though, if you want that."

"Sure."

It's in Bucktown, only a few blocks from where Pat lives.

"By the way, what's Artie's last name?"

"It's Thompson. Like the governor."

"Edgar's the governor now. Thompson stepped down, finally."

"What's the difference? They're all a bunch of crooks." Jerry lets out a short laugh and I hear phlegm making its first appearance of the day in his throat. "You know, there's something I've been meaning to tell you."

"What's that?"

"I can't remember what it was." He laughs again. "It's not important. It'll come to me sometime."

"Probably sometime when you're a little more awake."

"Yeah, you said it."

I try directory assistance while I flip to the front of the paper, to Charlotte Penske's column. I always read that last, though it's the thing most people read first. The operator says there's no listing for an Arthur or A. Thompson on Wabansia. I'm about to ask for the numbers of any A. Thompsons regardless of street address when an item in the POISON PENSKES section of Charlotte's column catches my eye. It startles me so much that I hang up the phone.

"Frankie!" I shout to her before I'm done reading the item. That makes me lose my place and I have to start over:

> IS THE SPECTER OF POLICE HARASSMENT
> REARING ITS UGLY HEAD AGAIN?
> The Poison Pen hears it could very well be. Two of Area 5's finest paid a visit to Phil Moony, the former city paramedic who many believe was set up by police four years ago in a political revenge scheme. Moony's wife, Frankie Martin, says the pair was "rude and crude." C'mon, guys, can't you find some real crooks to bother?

Frankie enters the kitchen just as I finish. "What do you want?" Her face brightens in surprise as I hold up the paper. "Did she run something? I can't believe it!"

"You can't? I can. If you talked to her about it, which you obviously did, how can you possibly think she wouldn't run something?"

Frankie shakes her head. "That's not what I mean. I knew she was going to run something, I just can't believe she got it into this morning's paper. She must've phoned it in when she went to the women's room."

"I thought you promised you weren't going to say anything to her."

"I know. But I thought about it and changed my mind."

"So you think this is a good thing?"

"Move over, let me read it."

"I'll give you all the room you want."

Frankie breaks into a grin as she finishes.

"So you like it?" I say.

"Are you kidding? I *love* it."

"Well, I hate it."

She picks up the phone. "I've got to call Charlotte."

I put the phone back on the receiver. "Frankie, did you hear me?"

She nods. "Yeah, you said you hate it."

"Doesn't that mean anything to you?"

"Yeah." She smiles and picks up the phone again. "It means you're wrong."

"I'm wrong? You've got to be kidding."

"No, I'm not, Phil. You should feel lucky to have the press on your side. Very few people have that privilege."

"I don't care about the press, I care about the cops. And this"—I lift the paper up and toss it back down—"is only going to piss them off."

"Well, big deal. So the police get pissed off. What's the difference? Mad or not, we already know they're out to get you. So all we've done is fire a preemptive strike in the war of public opinion. Maybe it won't do any good. But it can't do any harm. Think about it for a minute."

I do. I give it almost two minutes, as a matter of fact. And I'm just about ready to come around to Frankie's way of seeing things. And then the phone rings.

Frankie answers it. I can tell by her response that it's our attorney, Burt Levison. From listening a few seconds, I can tell he's read Charlotte Penske's column. I grab a pen and write a note on the front page of the paper: *I'M NOT HOME!* I hold it under Frankie's nose until she nods, then go upstairs to take a shower.

* * *

Frankie's just getting off the phone when I get back downstairs. I give her my best I-told-you-so smile. "So it can't do any harm, huh? What did Burt have to say?"

"That wasn't Burt. I hung up with him a few minutes ago. I promised I'd have you call him. He just wants to know what's going on. He thinks it's a bad idea to talk to the police without him being there. After that, Pat called. He thought it was a terrific item. He says Vic Rosten probably shit his shorts, pardon my French, when he saw it. That's a quote."

"Which part's a quote?"

"The whole thing: shit his shorts, pardon my French." She smiles. "I also heard from Tim Rayburn, the guy from the *Tribune* who wrote that nice story about you that time. And just now, that was your old friend Dana Stearns."

"Who's he?"

"She. You were dating her when you started dating me. Remember?"

"Oh yeah, Dana. I wasn't still dating her."

"She thought you were."

"Oh, that's right." Dana followed Frankie home one night and advised her to lay off me. It was the first and only time I've ever had two women vying for my affection. They almost came to blows. "Did she say how she's doing?"

"Fan*tas*tic." Frankie treats me to a breathy imitation. "She's an attorney now, you know. And she wanted me to tell you that if you need any counsel, she'd be happy to represent you, pro bono."

"How thoughtful." I smile. "Maybe I'll give her a call."

"Don't you dare." She shakes her head. "I'm not sure what amazes me more: how many people we know, or how many people read Charlotte's column."

"I'm amazed by both."

I call Pat and get his reaction to the news about the other Phil Moony. He's as baffled as we are, but he has a couple of questions off the top of his head: Where did Moony die? Who found him? I don't know, but I promise to try to find out at tonight's wake. He knows it would be inappropriate to accompany us to that, but he's pretty insistent on coming to see Artie with me. I tell him it's not necessary. But considering Artie's a big dude who may be a cop, I am feeling a mite bit chickenshit about going alone. So I don't mind having my arm twisted.

I fail in my efforts to persuade Frankie to stay out of the house. She insists that it's important to have someone near the phone in case Larry Little calls. She also reassures me that she's armed and dangerous.

When I get to Artie's, I see Pat already parked a few houses down the street. He pries himself out of his shiny new car while I park my rusty old one. We meet at the curb and head up the walk together.

"I've got a little bad news," he says.

"What's that?"

"My retired lab guy. It turns out he took permanent retirement last year."

"Where'd he go?"

"My, aren't you quick today." Pat points one thumb at the sky, one at the ground. "One of two places."

"Oh, I get it." I shake my head. "I am feeling kind of brain-dead."

"That's nothing." Pat laughs. "It turns out I went to the guy's funeral."

Artie lives on the second floor of a brick two-flat. We conclude that from checking over the top doorbell, where Thompson/Shrum is printed on a strip of masking tape. Shortly after I ring it, I hear footsteps coming down the stairs. They belong to a tall slender woman with straight black hair, a small tight mouth and thin lips. She's wearing a purple-and-blue Indian-print dress. If it didn't have such bad connotations these days, I'd say she looks like a hippie. She doesn't open the door but we can see her through the window in the top half.

I tell Pat I think she could be Artie's girlfriend. The only trouble with that is she looks nothing like the woman I saw going into the hockey game last night.

"What's her name?"

"Good question." I'm sure Artie's mentioned it, but I tend to tune him out when he rattles on. The only thing I remember about her is that she makes jewelry.

"Can I help you with something?" She's eying us suspiciously and I don't blame her.

"Jenny?" It comes to me suddenly when I think about what she does for a living. When Artie first told me, I thought they sounded like the perfect couple: Artie the Artist and Jenny the Jeweler.

"Yes?" She still sounds suspicious.

I start to explain how I know Artie. To my surprise, she knows exactly who I am.

"Oh yes, hello." She opens the door a crack. "How was the hockey game?"

That catches me off guard. "Oh, it was great." I figure lying is the path of least resistance here. I hope she doesn't ask for any details. I don't even remember what team the Hawks were playing. "I take it Artie isn't home."

"No, he's in the Apple. I thought you knew that. That's why he gave you his hockey tickets."

"Well yes, I did know that, but . . ." I pause a moment, realizing how odd what I'm about to say might sound. "You see, I thought I saw Artie at the game last night."

She shakes her head. "I don't think so. Not unless he's figured out a way to be in two places at once. Artie's pretty clever, but he's not that clever."

We all nod in admiration of Artie's cleverness for an uncomfortable moment, then I ask Jenny exactly what it is Artie does for a living.

"He's a graphic designer. You didn't know that?"

"Of course, that's right." I was hoping for something a bit more graphic but I don't press her.

She gives me a quizzical look. "Is something wrong?"

"No, it's nothing. It's just that I was supposed to get his mail and put it in his office, but the key he gave me doesn't work."

"You wouldn't happen to have an extra one, would you?" Pat asks.

"Uh, no, I wouldn't." I'm about 75 percent sure she's lying and 150 percent sure I don't blame her.

Pat nods. "Do you have a number where he can be reached?"

"I don't have a number, but I know the name of it. He's staying at the Chelsea Hotel. Do you know if that's the one where Sid Vicious killed Nancy?"

Pat and I look at each other and exchange full shrugs.

"Yeah, I think it is." Jenny answers her own question.

"Well, I'm sorry to just drop by like this," I say. "But I was positive I saw Artie last night and I need to talk to him. Since there's no listing in the phone book, I—"

"Sure there is. We're both listed, as a matter of fact."

"You are? I guess the operator must've missed it."

"That doesn't surprise me. But as far as Artie being at the game, that's impossible. He called last night from SoHo."

I'm not about to argue with Jenny. Who knows how much she knows about her boyfriend? I'm half tempted to tip her off that he took a blonde to the game, but now I'm not so sure it was Artie. "Well I guess it was a guy who looked just like him. Sorry to bother you."

"That's all right. When Artie calls, I'll tell him you were looking for him. He's supposed to be home tomorrow. As far as his mail goes, I wouldn't worry about it. All he gets are bills anyway."

"So," I say to Pat as we start down the walk, "I guess that leaves us with a few questions."

He nods. "Starting with whether she was telling the truth."

"And what do you think about that?"

"Ryan votes nay. What about you?"

"I'm inclined to believe her."

"You've always been a sucker for scrawny dark-haired dames

with no makeup or personality. But where do you stand on the big question?''

''Which one's that?''

''Who's Sid Vicious?''

''I think you better ask your nephew about that one.''

An ill-advised breakfast at a yuppie diner in Bucktown leaves us both feeling a little ill. After that, I head to the office and Pat heads off to check on some things.

He's trying to determine whether Artie Thompson is a Chicago PD narc and whether Purple Haze, the Rush Street nightclub Larry Little told me about, ever really existed. My first chore is to call the Chelsea Hotel.

For some reason, I'm not at all surprised to learn there's nobody named Thompson staying there. I don't bother asking the clerk if this is where Sid Vicious killed Nancy. Her voice is so weak and distant, she sounds like she's been the victim of a vicious beating herself. Now I'm more inclined to believe Jenny Shrum is being truthful about Artie. If she were covering for him, I doubt she'd be so willing to give out information that could be so easily checked and found to be wrong. But Pat didn't trust her, and he's been doing this a lot longer and better than I have.

I check the phone book. Like Jenny said, the number's listed under her name. But I still can't find it under Artie's. I call and get Jenny. She doesn't sound pleased to be hearing back from me so soon. She sounds even less pleased when I tell her Artie's not at the Chelsea like she said.

"I'm sorry, you must be mistaken."

"No, Jenny, I'm not. And I don't think I'm mistaken about seeing Artie at the Stadium last night either."

"That's impossible."

"Are you sure?"

"Of course I'm sure. I thought we went over all this when you came barging over here this morning."

"I'm sorry if we barged, but this is important. I saw Artie at the game last night. He was with a blonde woman in a fur coat. This morning you said he was staying at—"

"What are you telling me? Are you trying to tell me something?" Her voice gets louder with each question. "Who put you up to this? Is this some kind of joke? Because if it is, it's not funny!"

"No, it's no joke. I'm trying to find—"

"Fuck you! Fuck you! Okay?"

"Okay." I barely get that out before she slams down the phone. Now I'm positive Pat was wrong about Jenny not telling the truth. I feel bad for upsetting her, but I don't think it would do any good to call back and apologize. So it goes. You can't be loved by all of the people all of the time.

I decide to head downstairs and check the mail, mine and Artie's. I may not have the key to his office, but I do have the key to his mailbox. At least I think it's his.

It is. If today's any indication, Artie gets lots of mail. Much more than I do, and more than Jenny said. There are bills, sure, but there's also a foot-high stack of catalogs and magazines. Artie's clearly into sports in a big way. He gets *Sports Illustrated, The Sporting News,* and *Hockey News.* He even gets *Chicago Sports Profiles.* But as I stand in the lobby sorting through the pile, the thing that attracts my attention is a postcard that flutters out of the pile. It's an invitation to a sports-card collectors' show in Merrillville, Indiana, next month.

It's revealing to find out Artie's into card collecting. But what's more interesting is that the invitation is addressed to Richard D. Thompson. I quickly sort through the other mail. Although there are the typically odd misspellings that occur when junk mail companies start passing your name around like a bad cold, I now see why I couldn't find a phone listing for Artie. It's such a revelation that I announce it out loud to myself.

"His name's not Artie, it's *R.D.*"

"Hey, Phil, what's up?"

It's a good thing I'm downstairs in the lobby, otherwise I might go right through the roof. I'm so startled to hear my name called out that my feet actually leave the floor. In the time it takes me to whirl around, I think about dropping the mail and grabbing the gun out of my pocket. I don't do either.

I also think about how vulnerable I'd be if someone wanted to attack me. That thought makes me shiver.

I expect to see Artie. Excuse me, *R.D.* But even though I've been looking for him, I'm relieved it's not him. It's my neighbor, Mitch Michaels.

He raises his hands apologetically. "Whoa, Phil, sorry to scare you."

"That's okay."

He grins. "So, what's bugging you?"

"Nothing. I'm just a little jumpy today. What are you doing here?"

"I'm just working in the neighborhood, I thought I'd drop by. You know, say hi."

It's only when Mitch mentions working that I notice the insecticide smell that so annoys Frankie about him. This is maybe the fourth time he's stopped to see me. Once we ended up going to lunch, but mostly he just likes to stay long enough to get a shot of booze. I think it would be fair to say that Mitch has a drinking problem.

He wants to know if I want to grab some lunch. I tell him about my late breakfast and invite him upstairs for a few minutes. When we get there, I notice he's got the *Sun-Times* under his arm.

He unfolds it and holds it up. "I read this thing in the paper about you, Phil. That's pretty cool."

I shake my head. "No, it's not, Mitch. You don't ever want the cops hassling you."

"No, not that part. I mean having your name in the paper and all." He smiles. "Being a celebrity."

"Take it from me: That kind of celebrity you don't want."

He nods. "Yeah, I can understand that. I've had run-ins with the cops. Nothing like what you've been through, of course." He holds up the paper again. "I didn't realize who you were until I read this. I remember reading about you back when it was going on. It was because of supporting Mayor Harold that they went after you, right?"

"Well, sort of. It was more complicated than that."

He shakes his head. "Man, the city started going downhill when he died."

"Yeah, I agree." I'm surprised, and pleasantly, to hear Mitch say that. I watch as his eyes do the whole circuit of the office. They pause on the coffeepot. It's right next to where I usually keep the booze. "I'd offer you a drink, but I'm out."

"Oh no, that's okay, don't worry about it. I never drink before lunch."

"Someone broke in here and stole all my booze."

"You're kidding."

"No I'm not."

"Was it the cops?"

"I don't know. I guess it could've been."

"So what is it they're busting your chops about this time? Is there anything I can help you with? Lawyer, whatever?"

I wave my hand in a dismissal. "Nah, it's really nothing. They were just asking me about something that happened down the street here in the Milshire Hotel."

"Oh, great place."

"You've been in there?"

He nods. "That's one of our buildings. They're a three-bagger."

"What's that?"

"Rats, roaches and 'Ricans."

"Yeah, I've been in places like that." I start to tell him about the time I was on a call to an apartment where four Puerto Rican kids were hanging out, teenagers. We got the call because one of them collapsed. I got him revived with an ammonia cap. Inhaling ammonia is not a pleasant experience, believe me. When he came around, he had a tremor, shaking his head like crazy. One of the kids thought he'd gotten a buzz off it. He thought it was a popper. So he asked me to try some. Well, he didn't really ask, he just grabbed it out of my hand. And of course he had a tremor, and each of the other kids thought he was getting a buzz, so each of them inhaled it. I just stood there dumbfounded. But I must've been smiling a bit. Because one of them asked me, "Hey man, why didn't you tell us?" And I said, "Because you didn't give me a goddamn chance to."

The phone rings before I can get to the part in the story where the kids start passing the cap. I put up my hand to excuse myself, then pick it up.

"Good morning, asshole."

I don't say anything.

"You know who this is, don't you?"

"I've got a pretty good idea."

"You want to take a guess?"

"I'm not in the mood for guessing, Larry."

"I figured you'd remember me." He laughs. It's smaller and higher-pitched than the guy who called the night before last.

"Yeah, I do. There's only one thing, Larry."

"What's that?"

"You're not the same Larry I talked to the other night."

"What do you mean?"

"I mean your voice is different." It sounds as if he's squeezing his nose with his fingers.

"Yeah, well I had a few drinks the other night. Right now I'm sober as a judge."

"That's not what I'm talking about." I glance up and catch Mitch's attention. He's pretending to be reading the paper, but I'm sure he's taking in everything I'm saying. That's what I do when I'm in someone's office. "Hold on a second, will you?" I cover the receiver with my hand and apologetically ask Mitch to leave. He nods and gets up quickly. I wait until he's out the door before getting back on the line.

"So, what do you mean?" Larry Little sounds indignant, like someone who's just been given a tip on oral hygiene.

"What's the matter, Larry? Isn't your brain working today? I already told you: You're *not* the same guy as the other night."

"Yes I am."

"Fine, whatever you say. Do you want to tell me why you're calling or do you want to waste the whole day bullshitting me?"

"I think you know why I'm calling."

"I think you should tell me." I doubt my phone is tapped, but he could be running a tape recorder. Either way, I'm not going to say anything that could be construed as incriminating.

"Did you find the present I left you?"

"What do you think?"

He laughs. "Yeah, I think you did. Are you happy with it?"

"I'm tickled to fucking death. Why don't you just get to the point."

"Okay, okay. You sound like you're in a bad mood, dude. That should be me. After all, I'm the one that got stiffed. I bet you felt pretty clever pulling that stunt switching the briefcase."

"Outwitting you isn't terribly demanding, Larry."

"Oh yeah? Too bad you can't ask Tony Rio about that." He laughs. "But that's okay, I don't mind. I guess I owe you one, for breaking into your house and all. Anyway, we need to have a meet. You've got something I want, I'm willing to pay generously for it."

"More generous than you've been so far, I hope."

"Oh yeah, sure. Don't worry, Phil. There's going to be plenty for all of us."

"Just how many of *us* are there, Larry?"

He laughs again, but he sounds nervous. I'm sure he didn't want to give that away. "Less than there used to be. We should have a meet soon. How's tonight look?"

"Sorry, I've got a wake to go to. It's for a guy named Moony. Does that ring any bells?"

He laughs. "Yeah, lots of them."

"Tomorrow would be much better. Let's make it afternoon.

I've got to get an appraisal done first. And you never know. I may want to talk to the cops about the break-in at my house."

"Now come on, Phil. Don't do anything stupid. You play ball here and things could turn out very nice. All you got to do is name the place. You're holding the cards."

For some reason I'm suddenly inclined to believe this guy, whoever he is. As Pat said, if the idea was to get me into trouble, the cops would have been on my ass the minute I stepped out of the Milshire. Maybe it's wishful thinking, but right now I believe someone may have merely decided to use me as a courier. If I hadn't seen the guy in my office, maybe he would've knocked me on the head and taken the briefcase. Or maybe he would've smiled, handed me the $500 and told me to have a nice life.

"Three o'clock tomorrow," I say. "At a bar called the Irish Wolfhound. On Milwaukee Avenue, west side of the street, two blocks south of Six Corners. You know where it is?"

"I'll find it. How will I know you?"

That's a strange question. Is the guy bullshitting, or does he really not know what I look like?

"That's easy," I say. "I'll be the only other guy at the bar."

"Okay. Be sure to bring the cards with you."

"Cards? What cards?"

19

I haven't gotten to first base in my efforts to locate R. D. Thompson, but I don't have any trouble finding Home Plate, the card shop Dave Ginther told me about. It's a tiny storefront at the end of a row of tiny storefronts connected by a single red awning to form a block of downtown Morton Grove, a metropolis that spans maybe four blocks in all.

I've brought along a handful of cards for an appraisal. But as I pull into a metered parking space and appraise the shop from the curb, I see a hand-printed sign taped to the door. The sign tells me there's really no point in getting out of the car. I get out anyway to have a closer look:

CLOSED DUE TO DEATH IN THE FAMILY

That's all it says. There's no indication how long it's been closed or when it will reopen.

The reflection of the sunlight makes it hard to see through the windows. Using my hands as a visor, I'm able to glimpse several rows of cards neatly lined up under a glass counter. I can't make out any of the prices on the white stickers beside them.

I decide to drop by the pharmacy next door and see if I can get any information about the card shop. I'm curious to find out who died. As I turn onto the sidewalk, I see someone coming about fifty yards away who makes me keep right on walking. It's a guy I haven't seen in two years, a guy I don't want to see for another twenty. It's my old friend Ron Ostrow, the guy who asked me to score half an ounce of dope for him a few years ago.

Ostrow sees me. I know he does. I know because he does an immediate about-face and begins walking away real quickly. He keeps his head down and speeds up, not looking back. When he reaches the corner, he turns right, still not looking back.

I start to give chase. Seeing Ostrow here, so close to the shop where someone has recently died, makes me very suspicious. The fact that the shop was recommended by Dave Ginther, who knows both of us, makes me even more suspicious. I consider Dave a friend, but I've seen too many friendships end over the years to count on that.

Halfway down the block I pull up. If Ostrow wants to get past me, he'll probably cut over on the next street or through the alley that runs behind the stores. I turn and sprint in the other direction, rounding Home Plate again as I turn the corner. I stop near the back of the building and sneak a glance down the alley. About two-thirds of the way down the block, I see Ostrow coming my way.

I duck in behind a cement post that juts out of the back of the store. This keeps me hidden from view, both down the alley and along the side street. When Ostrow gets about ten feet away, I step out. I aim my gun at his head.

He pulls to a dead stop. His mouth opens so wide I can almost see the back of his throat. "No, please!"

"What the fuck are you doing here?" I motion with the gun for him to move into the hiding space.

He obeys, backing up. "Nothing, I was just—"

"Bullshit." I start toward him, still holding the gun.

He puts up his hands. "I swear, Phil, I was just coming to this store and—"

"Which store?"

"Home Plate, it's a baseball shop. Then I saw you and I—"

"And you started to run away."

He nods. "Yeah, that's right, I started to run away."

"Why?"

"I was afraid you'd see me. The last time you saw me . . . well, you remember."

I do. Of course I do. I nod. I can't help but smile. That was the only time in my life that I had the satisfaction of really beating someone up. Sure, I've gotten into a few fights, slugged and been slugged. But this was much different. This was on a whole other level. This was domination. It was being in a situation where I could've beaten another human being to a bloody pulp, beaten him to death, if I wanted to. There was a pleasure about it that I haven't experienced before or since. Of course there was also something shameful and dark about it. It's a side of myself I don't ever want to see again.

"Do you expect me to believe it's just coincidence that you're coming to this card shop?" I ask.

Ostrow looks baffled. It's a baffling question if you don't know what's going on. I can't tell if he does. He could be pretending not to.

"I guess so, I don't know," he says.

"Do you know a guy named R. D. Thompson?"

He shakes his head.

"What about Tony Rio?"

"No."

"Larry Little?"

"No." Ostrow's hands are shaking. He's still holding them up. "Listen, Phil, I swear, I've never heard of these guys. I read in the paper today that the cops are hassling you again. But that's the only thing I know. I swear, that's all I know. I've got nothing to do with it."

"Then what the hell are you doing up here?"

"I came to get something appraised." He begins to lower one hand cautiously. I nod to allow him to continue. He reaches into the pocket of his coat and pulls out a bulging envelope. "Cards. The 'fifty-nine White Sox. They're all autographed. I've had them since I was a kid. That's the year they won the pennant." He holds the envelope out for me to look. I don't bother.

"So why'd you come to this place?"

"A guy at work told me about it."

"Who? Dave Ginther?"

He nods. "Yeah, how'd you know?"

I don't bother to answer. I back away a step, still pointing the gun at his head. "If you're setting me up again, Ostrow, I'll break every fucking bone in your body."

"I swear I'm not."

I gesture with the gun for him to leave. He still has one hand up. "Don't you dare tell anyone you ran into me. Understand?"

"Sure, Phil, whatever you say. I'm sorry."

Maybe I should be the one to apologize—but I don't. It could all be a coincidence, but I'm still not sure.

"The store's closed today," I say. "Somebody died."

He nods anxiously. He backs down the alley until he's about twenty feet away. Then he turns and starts off slowly, looking over his shoulder every few seconds. I just stand there watching him. When he gets about three-quarters of the way down the block, he yells, "You're a fucking crazy asshole, Moony!" Then he starts to run.

I don't bother to respond. If it is all a coincidence, he's right. If it's not and he's up to something, I'll get my chance for payback later. You can count on it.

I drive straight home. Before going inside, I stop next door at the garage and put the cards back in their hiding place with the others. As soon as I get in the door, Frankie thrusts the phone at me as if there's a tarantula crawling on it.

In a way there is. It's our attorney, Burt Levison. I tell Frankie I don't want to talk to him, but she says she's spoken to him twice already today and now it's my turn.

"Don't you have something you want to talk to me about?" he asks.

"Yeah, I do. I'd like to find out if you know the difference between a lawyer and a carp."

"What? What are you talking about?"

"One's a bottom-feeding scumsucker, the other's a fish."

"Very funny, Phil. Very fucking funny."

"Yeah, I thought you'd like it."

"But I'm serious. If you've got the police talking to you, you should be talking to me, not the newspapers."

"That was my wife, Burt. Far as I'm concerned, I don't feel like talking to any of you. But I'll tell you what: Of the three, you're at the top of my list. How's that?"

I don't wait for an answer before hanging up. As soon as I do, Frankie fills me in on what she's been up to. For starters she's learned that Phil Moony lived on Willow Road in Winnetka. She's also found out that he owned a sports memorabilia shop on Dempster Street in Morton Grove.

"Is that right? Well, that explains why the place was closed today. A sign on the door said there'd been a death in the family."

"It also explains why the currency you're dealing in is baseball cards. You want to know what else I learned? Tony Rio was convicted of manslaughter in nineteen seventy-four. He served ten years in Stateville."

"That's weird. When Larry Little called the other night, he implied that Rio had just gotten out of the joint."

"Recidivistic tendencies, perhaps. He probably got himself back in again. Out in New Jersey. Isn't that where you said his driver's license was from?"

"Yeah, that's right."

The phone rings. Frankie begs me to get it, saying she's been swamped with calls. I could tell her it's her own fault for blabbing to Charlotte Penske, but that would make me a real cad.

It's Pat Ryan calling in with a report. I can tell from his tone that he hasn't had this much fun since he retired.

"Far as I can tell, there's nobody named Artie Thompson in the CPD."

"I found out his name isn't Arthur. It's R-period. D-period."

"Yeah, I know, I found that out too."

"How?"

"I checked the damn phone book under Thompson until I

found one on Wabansia. You don't have to be a rocket scientist to do this work, you know. So it looks like his old lady was telling the truth about something after all."

"Well, he wasn't." I tell Pat about my call to the Chelsea Hotel and follow-up with R.D.'s girlfriend, Jenny. I also tell him about the card show invitation I found in R.D.'s mail.

"You're going to that wake tonight, right?"

"Right."

"Well, tomorrow, then, you and me will have a look inside R.D.'s office."

"That sounds fine to me. But it's got to be the morning." I tell him about my afternoon appointment with my latest caller named Larry Little.

"Whoever the guy is, you can be sure he's not the real Larry Little."

"Why do you say that?"

"I did some checking on the Purple Haze nightclub. It turns out the place definitely did exist. And the guy who called the other night was telling something of the truth. The controlling partner in the joint *was* Phil Moony. But the manager of the place wasn't Larry Little. It was a guy named Karl Mitchell. Does that ring any bells with you?"

"No, it doesn't. How'd you find that out?"

"Sources and records. Some people have great memories. And if you look in the right place, there's always something on paper. But here's the interesting part: The Purple Haze closed down in 'seventy-three, shortly after a fatal shooting. The guy who did the shooting was the bouncer in the place. You want to know what his name was?"

"Tony Rio?"

"Shit, how'd you know that?"

"My wife did some checking herself."

"Is that so? Well did she tell you who the guy he killed was?"

"No, she didn't."

"He was the bartender in the joint. His name was Larry Little."

"No shit."

"Yeah, no shit is right."

20

Winnetka is the paradigm of fine suburban living. It's the cleanest, the ritziest, the tidiest, the safest. But every once in a while it suddenly gets weirdest.

Like four years ago, when a baby-sitter named Laurie Dann went over the edge and shot up an elementary school. Or two years ago, when a New Trier High School student named David Biro broke into a young couple's town house and shot them to death just for the hell of it.

On that one, the cops came up with the theory that the murders were a terrorist hit by the Irish Republican Army. The sister of the woman who got murdered was a lawyer who'd worked in Belfast. But she had done free legal work for the IRA. Even after Laurie Dann's spree, the Winnetka cops apparently couldn't believe one of their own could commit such an atrocity. Although the kid was a known troublemaker who'd been spotted a block away on the night of the murders, they never got around to questioning him. The only reason they caught him—over a year after the murders—was because he bragged about it and one of his friends ratted him out.

Since Frankie has the address, we take a ride past the late Phil Moony's house on our way to his wake. It turns out he lived in a modest split level on the "poor" side of Winnetka, west of the commuter train tracks and over toward the Edens Expressway. As we drive by, Frankie comments on how nice the three crab apple trees in the front yard will look when they bloom. My attention is focused on the three cars parked in the driveway. One of them is a red Fiero. I turn around on the next block and ask Frankie to get out a pen and paper. As we approach the Moony residence again, I slow almost to a stop so I can read the plate number to her.

It's not necessary. Anyone could remember STRIKE 3.

"I have a friend in the Secretary of State's office who can trace that," I say.

"Who doesn't?" Frankie smiles. She always smiles when she insults me. Unless she's mad. Then she glowers in an effort to add injury.

We have a leisurely dinner at a forgettable steak joint in Northbrook before heading to the funeral home. It's located across from a sprawling barnyard of a bar that features unlimited free chicken wings during happy hour. A message on the towering sign board indicates that they're bringing back disco music on weekends. Or maybe it never went away out here.

There are about a dozen cars in the parking lot of the funeral home. The red Fiero is right near the main door. We pause for a look in the window to see if it gives a clue to its owner's personality. But it's new and free of the telltale clutter in my car that reveals so much about mine.

"Do you think this is the car that was following you?" Frankie asks.

"I'd be willing to bet on it. I'd also be willing to bet it belonged to Phil Moony."

"Or one of his kids."

The viewing for Moony is in the West Parlor. We pause in the lobby to collect our thoughts. My idea for coming here is to pick up any scuttlebutt we can about Moony or how he died. But we don't want to be obtrusive. I've never read Emily Post, but I'm sure crashing a wake would be near the top of her list of faux pas. I'd figured that if anyone asked why we came, we'd say we were extending condolences on behalf of Larry Little. Now that we know he's been dead for twenty years, that no longer seems appropriate.

"Are you sure you're ready for this?" I ask Frankie.

She shrugs. "Are *you* ready is the question. This is minor league compared to some of the uncomfortable situations I got into as a reporter. Back then I had to be a major league jerk."

We move to the doorway of the West Parlor and peer inside. There are maybe twenty people in the room, half of them sitting in folding chairs and the rest of them milling about. At the head of the room to the right of the coffin, a stunning blonde in a tight black wool dress is chatting with an elderly couple. She's flirting with fifty and there's a sag in her figure that gives her something of a fading matinee idol quality. But fifteen years back you can be certain she was drop-dead gorgeous.

"Based on what Little and Rio said, I'll bet that's Betty," I whisper to Frankie.

She nods and gives me a soft push. "We came this far, let's wing it."

As we start in, a voice behind me calls, "Hey, Phil."

I turn and see my landlord, Jerry Gabriel, walking toward me. I've never seen Jerry in anything but jeans and a turtleneck, so he looks out of place in a black Armani suit and tie. But he's still got a grand's worth of gold hanging from his neck. And of course he seems very out of place at a wake for a guy I don't even know.

I hold out my hand and we shake. "What are you doing here?" I ask.

"I was going to ask you the same question."

Frankie smiles. "He asked you first."

"This is my wife, Frankie. This is Jerry Gabriel, my landlord on Kedzie."

"It's a pleasure to meet you." Jerry cradles Frankie's right hand with both of his for a moment, then turns to me. "My girlfriend's father died. Remember when I said there was something I'd been meaning to tell you? That was it: You and Beth's dad had the same name."

"I'm sorry." Frankie and I say it in a duet.

"That's okay. We've only been going out a month or two. I barely knew the guy. But he used to be a baseball player back in the fifties or something. He had a sports-card shop in Morton Grove."

Jerry notices me nodding as he talks. "What am I telling you for? You probably already know this. How did you know Phil, Phil?"

I glance at Frankie, who shoots me a little smile. I decide to let Jerry in on things a bit.

"I don't. But a couple of nights ago I got a call from a guy in California who said he was a friend of his from years ago. He called our house by mistake. I told him I'd try to help him find Moony. Next thing I know, I see his obit in the paper."

"No shit. What was the guy's name?"

"Larry Little."

"Well, you should tell Betty. That's Beth's mother."

"I wouldn't want to bother her."

"Don't worry about it. She'll probably be glad to hear someone was asking about him."

Frankie and I exchange looks. I don't think Betty will be at all glad to meet someone who says a guy that's been dead for twenty years was asking about her husband.

"We probably shouldn't disturb her."

"Don't be ridiculous." Jerry begins scanning the crowd. "I'm just trying to find Beth. I know she's here. I saw her car parked right out in front."

"That wouldn't be the Fiero?"

"Yeah, that's right. Why?"

I shrug. "I was just curious. I noticed the plates."

Jerry smiles. "That was her father's idea. He had a Mercedes that said HOME RUN. Her mother's says BALL 4."

"How did Mr. Moony die?" Frankie asks.

"Heart attack. Dropped dead right in the shop."

"Was anybody there when it happened?"

"No. If they would've been they might have been able to call the paramedics and get his ticker restarted. A couple of kids found him. By then it was too late."

Jerry catches the attention of a pretty young blonde woman near the front of the room and she gives him a return wave. They start toward each other and Jerry motions for us to follow. Our paths cross at the first row of chairs.

From across the room Beth Moony looks like a socialite. She's been blessed with her mother's looks and shares her skill at filling out a mourning dress. But up close she barely looks old enough to drive.

We stand by awkwardly as they embrace.

"How are you holding up, Old Gal?" Jerry asks, hanging on to her hand.

She nods. "I'm doing all right. I'll be better when this business is over. It's hard seeing all these people. I don't know what to say to them."

"How about your mom? How's she doing?"

Beth glances toward her mother. "She had a few rough spots today, but other than that she's been a real trooper. It's Jason that I'm worried about."

Jerry nods. "Yeah, I didn't see him. Is he here?"

"No. He's still back at the house. He said he'd be here soon."

"I want you to meet someone," Jerry says. "Remember I told you about my friend with the same name as your father? This is him. Beth Moony, meet Phil Moony."

I hold out my hand. "I'm very sorry about your father. I'm sure it was a terrible shock."

"Yes, thank you." She nods, then looks at Frankie.

"And this is his wife . . ."

Frankie steps forward as Jerry's face goes blank. "Frankie Martin."

"Sorry," Jerry says. "I'm terrible with names."

"That's okay." Frankie takes Beth's hand. "I'm so sorry to be meeting you under these circumstances."

"I know. It's hard for everyone." Beth looks at me. "Did you know Dad?"

"No I didn't. I . . ."

Jerry gets me off the hook by explaining about my call from Larry Little. I have to prompt him because he forgets Little's name.

"And he only called two nights ago?" Beth shakes her head and her hair springs loose from one ear. "How weird. That's the day Dad died."

"Do you know the guy?" Jerry asks.

Her forehead folds into three perfectly centered lines. "No, I don't think so. We should ask Mom."

"That's okay," I say. "We really don't want to disturb her."

"Don't be silly. She'll be glad to get away from the Conrads." She smiles and lowers her voice to a whisper. "They drive her *totally* bonkers."

I turn to see that Betty is still chatting with the same couple. Now that we're closer I can see that she's not speaking, only nodding as they talk.

Beth gets her mother's attention. We move as a group toward her as she pulls away from the Conrads.

Betty speaks to Beth before acknowledging us. "Have you seen your brother?"

"No, not yet. Don't worry, he'll be here soon."

"I hope so. He better be."

Beth explains to her mother who we are. Unlike Jerry she remembers Larry Little's name.

"Oh yes, Larry," Betty says. "He's living in California now, isn't he?"

My jaw drops in disbelief while my head nods in affirmation. "He said he lived in L.A."

She shakes her head with a touch of wistfulness. "I haven't seen Larry in almost twenty years. How's he doing?"

"He was a little drunk when he called."

She chuckles. "Then he hasn't changed much."

"We're so sorry about your husband," Frankie says.

"Thank you, I know. And thank you for coming. That's really very thoughtful of you. Especially coming up from the city."

"It wasn't any trouble," I say.

"We're having some people back to the house later. If you'd like to come, you'd be very welcome."

"No, that's okay," I say. "I'm sure you've got your hands full."

Betty nods distractedly as she catches sight of someone behind me. "I do now."

I glance over my shoulder to see a heavyset blond guy walking toward us. Staggering toward us is more like it.

Betty moves ahead to meet him. "I hope you didn't drive here in that condition."

Beth follows her mother and Jerry looks unsure whether to follow Beth. He looks at us and I tell him we're on our way out.

"I'll walk you out. I could use some air." Jerry pulls a pack of Marlboros out of his shirt pocket.

"Is that Beth's brother?" I ask.

Jerry nods. "Older brother, Jason. He's taking things pretty hard. He and the old man weren't seeing eye-to-eye. Jason works at the shop. They had a fight about something and Jason decided to split. So he's feeling guilty wondering if his father would've died if he'd stayed around."

"That's real tough," Frankie says. "Do you know what they were fighting about?"

It strikes me as sort of an impudent question, but Jerry's a pretty rude dude himself. He just lets out a short laugh. "Beats me. Probably over whether to put the Reggie Jackson card on the top shelf of the display case. They were always arguing over things like that."

Jerry lights his cigarette as soon as we get outside. "So, did you manage to hook up with R.D.?"

"No, I couldn't get hold of him."

"Yeah, well I'd like to get ahold of his neck. The jerk owes me two months. I'm glad I've got you in that place, Phil. Otherwise I'd be looking down the barrel of a shotgun named Irving."

I've heard the line before but Frankie looks puzzled.

Jerry grins. "The Irving Bank and Distrust. They're holding the note on the building."

We leave Jerry standing in the lot, smoking his cigarette and stroking his chains.

"So," Frankie says, as soon as we start to pull away, "did you discover enough surprises for one lifetime this evening?"

"Yeah, I really expected Betty to be a brunette."

"No way. She had to be a blonde. They make better liars, you know."

"I know. You've told me that before."

"Now are you sure Larry Little is—"

"Dead?"

She nods.

"I'm positive. Pat said so. He wouldn't have gotten that wrong."

"So Betty definitely is lying."

"*Most* definitely."

"Do you think she had something to do with her husband's death?"

"I'd say that's a pretty fair assumption. Now it's my turn to ask you a question. What do you think of Jerry Gabriel?"

"Strip away the bad cologne, the gold chains and the greasy smile, and I think you've got a pure unadulterated sleazeball. I also think he's overplaying his relationship with you. Did you hear him tell Jailbait you were a 'friend' of his? Another thing: I think he went out of his way to overstate his dislike for R.D."

"Maybe. But he's always bitching to me about R.D."

"You know what one of the biggest surprises is?"

"What's that?"

"That Betty Moony wasn't at all surprised to see you. Someone tipped her off that we were going to be there."

"Jerry?"

"I'd say that's a very good guess."

"And who tipped off Jerry?"

"That's a very good question. Whoever it is, it has to be the same guy who called you today."

"I'd probably be willing to bet it was R.D."

"I think you could probably *bank* on it." She smiles. "And I don't mean the Irving Bank and Distrust."

21

We get home to find a note taped to the back door. The heading indicates that it came *From the Desk of K. MITCH MICHAELS.* It's tilted and off center, a sign that Mitch, like so many other red-blooded Americans, orders his stationery from the bowels of the Sunday paper.

"I knew there was something weird about him," Frankie says. "He's one of those middle-name guys. Maybe he'll challenge H. Ross Perot for president."

It's a very short note done in very big letters:

Urgent!
Come see me right away!
Mitch

As I tear the paper off the door, I see that it's been covering a hole in one of our French windows. It's in the pane closest to the lock, about the size of a baseball. I feel an immediate pain in my gut, like I've just been hit with a baseball.

"I think I know what's so urgent," I say.

"What?" Frankie leans forward to see. "Oh shit! Don't tell me someone broke into our house!"

I wheel around when I hear the back gate open. If I had the gun in my pocket I'd probably reach for it, but I've stupidly left it in the glove box of the car.

It's Mitch. He's panting. "I've been watching for you," he calls. "You wouldn't believe what happened." His head bobs as he catches his breath. "It was an hour and a half ago, maybe two. I'm taking out the garbage when I see a guy over here near the back steps. I called out thinking it was you, but the guy doesn't say anything. I'm pretty sure he heard me, though, so that seems kind of suspicious. So I walk out into the alley and come over to the gangway and I see him duck between the garage and the porch. I call out your name, louder this time, but there's no response. So now I know something's wrong.

"Well, I think about calling the cops. But you know, it'd take them two days to get here. So I tiptoe back over to my garage and get my gun out of the 'Vette." Mitch smiles in response to Frankie's frown. "I've got a Glock that I keep in this little compartment in the side panel. You know, just in case. Believe me, I go into some pretty weird neighborhoods sometimes. And the 'Vette really attracts attention."

Frankie is still frowning.

"Anyway, I come back across the alley real quietly and creep up the gangway. When I get to this corner here, I spin out like this." Mitch treats us to a reenactment that's right out of every bad TV cop show you've ever seen. "I say, 'Freeze, motherfucker!' "

"Cut the jive, Mitch. Just tell us what happened, for chrissakes." Frankie's running short on patience. I understand the feeling.

Mitch shrugs. "When I turn the corner, the guy's gone."

"What, were you surprised? He had all night to get away."

Mitch ignores Frankie, but he looks annoyed. I don't blame him. He's expecting gratitude and all he gets is grief. If I saw someone breaking into his house, I sure wouldn't try to play Kojak. I'd call the cops and sit back and wait. On the other hand, it's probably the most excitement Mitch has had in years. He'll be telling this story to his grandkids.

"So then I hear something back out in the alley," he says. "I race down the gangway and see a guy sprinting away. He must've slipped over into the Miglins' yard and gone out through their gate. I start chasing him, but he hops into a car up near the corner and drives away."

"Did you get a look at the car?" I ask.

He nods. "Pontiac Fiero. I could tell because they've got that cheater bar across the back."

"Was it red?" I ask.

"It could've been. It was too dark to get a good look at it. Most of them are. Why do you ask that?"

I shake my head. "It's much too complicated to explain."

Another time and Mitch wouldn't let a point like that go. But right now he's too charged up telling his own story to take much interest in ours. Besides, Frankie's asking him another question in her own gracious style.

"So I take it you didn't get a good look at the license plate."

Mitch shakes his head. "Like I said, it was dark."

"Then I'm sure you didn't get a good look at the intruder either."

"No, not really. He was pretty big, I can tell you that."

"Do you know if he was black or white?" I ask.

"White. I'm sure of that."

"But it was dark," Frankie says.

Mitch chuckles. "If he was black, I wouldn't have seen him at all, right?"

"Did you call the cops?" I ask.

"Uh-uh. I thought about it and Lydia said I ought to, but after that thing in the paper and all, I wasn't sure you'd want me to."

"You did the right thing," I say. "If the cops came, we'd be up all night filling out reports. We're better off waiting to see what's missing and then calling them tomorrow." I look at Frankie and take a deep breath. "So, are you ready to go inside and face the music?"

"I've been ready since we got here."

She holds the door open for me, but I take it and nod for her to go ahead. This isn't an act of gentility on my part, it's just that

I can tell Mitch would like to come in and I'm certain Frankie would let the door slam in his face.

As soon as we're inside I step into the lead. Based on what Mitch said, I'm almost positive no one is still in the house, but if someone is, I don't want Frankie to be the front line.

We hit the kitchen first. The drawers are pulled out and the doors to all the cabinets are open. Miraculously, nothing has spilled onto the floor. Not only that, but my Phil Moony baseball card is still in its place on the refrigerator.

The situation is the same throughout the first floor. In the dining room, the drawers and upper doors to the hutch are standing open, but the china that was passed down from Frankie's grandmother is still in place, neatly stacked. In the living room, the home entertainment center is intact. The coffee tables have been shifted, but nothing else is out of place. It appears that we had a very considerate burglar.

Upstairs it's a different story but it's hardly Armageddon. The drawers to our dressers have been pulled out and emptied, with most of the contents ending up on the floor.

"Jesus Christ!" Frankie says.

Mitch holds out his hand in sympathy. "Our apartment got hit when we lived down in DePaul. Lydia said it felt just like she'd been raped."

Frankie closes her eyes for a moment and bites her lip. I move close to hold her hand. "It's going to be okay," I say.

She nods but doesn't say anything.

"Better check your jewelry," Mitch says. "That's the first thing these dirtbags go for."

"I don't have much jewelry. I'm a woman of peasant tastes." She manages a smile but it's a fragile one. If she stares at her underwear strewn over the floor for too long, I'm sure she'll break into tears. I steer her out of the room to prevent that from happening.

"It looks like someone was looking for something," Mitch says as we go back down the stairs.

"I don't think they came to borrow a cup of sugar," Frankie replies.

Before heading to the basement, I get a couple of Old Styles out of the refrigerator and hand one to Mitch. Frankie wants one too, even though she doesn't usually drink beer. When I get hers, I remember the shotgun behind the refrigerator. I chance a glance and see that it's still there.

Frankie stays upstairs to check her office while Mitch and I explore below. The rec room is a wreck, but that has more to do with my aversion to cleanliness than the efforts of our home invader. My work area is the hardest hit, with books and tools knocked off the shelves and the drawers to my filing cabinets hanging open, with files scattered on the floor.

"Looks like he got my radio and my cassette player," I say. This isn't true, but I want to discourage Mitch from the notion that someone came looking for something in particular. I sort through the contents of my desk drawers, in a heap on the floor. "And I think he got my pot."

"Yeah, the assholes always steal your dope," Mitch says.

When we get back up to the kitchen, Frankie says, "They cleaned out our cash stash." I can tell she's speaking for Mitch's benefit too. We don't have a cash stash.

"How much was there?" he asks.

"That depends on how recently my husband raided the bank," she says, looking at me.

I shrug. "About two hundred bucks the last time I looked."

Mitch slams his fist onto the countertop. "What a pisser. I wish I'd've nabbed the dirtbag."

"Don't worry about it," I said. "We appreciate the fact that you tried."

"Yes," Frankie adds. "You could've gotten hurt. That would've been far worse than losing money."

Mitch shrugs. "Phil would've done the same thing for me."

I don't want to touch that line and I don't have to, because the phone starts ringing.

I move down the hall to get it. If it's someone calling himself Larry Little, as I'm almost sure it is, I intend to unload on him. When I do, I want to be out of earshot of Mitch.

"Phil?" The voice on the line sounds far away but I know it's close by. One syllable is all it takes to recognize Lydia's mousy tone. She has a classic Chicago accent. All sounds come out through the nose. In her case it's the smallest nose I've ever seen. She's a small woman, clearing five feet only when she's wearing hooker heels. Frankie sometimes refers to her as Lydia Bug in honor of Mitch's profession. "Is he still over there?" she asks.

"Yes, you want to speak to him?"

"No, that's all right, I just wanted to know if he was there."

"You want me to send him home?"

"Well, if you're sure you don't need him."

"No, that's okay."

"I would've come over but I'm in the middle of giving myself a home permanent." Lydia is probably the only woman I've seen in twenty years who puts her hair in curlers, certainly the only woman under fifty who does so. "Is Frankie all right?"

"Yes, she's doing fine."

"Did they take a lot of stuff?"

"Not that much, considering."

"Well, be sure and write down every last thing you can think of for the insurance company. They'll try to jew you down every step of the way."

I thank Lydia for the advice and promise to send Mitch right home. "That was your ball and chain," I say when I get to the kitchen. "She'd like you back in your cell."

"Yeah, what else is new?"

"It is getting late," Frankie says. "And she's probably nervous if there's a burglar in the neighborhood."

As Mitch begins to move toward the door, I put out my hand. "We'll be sure to let you know what the cops say. And thanks for all you did. I really appreciate it."

"It was nothing. Like I said, you would've done the same for me. That's what being neighbors is all about."

I pick up the phone.

"Who are you calling? Pat?" Frankie asks.

I nod as I start to punch the numbers on the handset.

"Who's that?" Mitch asks, pausing at the door.

"A friend of ours who used to be a cop," I reply.

Mitch looks surprised. "You've got friends who are cops?"

"A few. Mostly ex-cops." I give Mitch a little wave to send him on his way.

The phone rings four times before Pat answers. His voice is more gravelly than usual.

"I woke you up, didn't I? Sorry."

"No no, that's all right. I just dozed off on the couch." He chuckles, and a whole truckload of gravel comes up. "I was watching 'Car 54, Where Are You?' " I hear him light a cigarette. "So, how was the wake?"

"Interesting, very interesting. I'll tell you all about it tomorrow. The reason I'm calling now is to let you know someone broke into our house."

"You're shitting me."

"Nope. Wish I was."

"How the hell did they get in?"

"Broke the window in the door, then reached in and turned the key on the inside latch."

"What, you left it in? You're not supposed to do that."

"I know, I know." I don't bother telling him it was Frankie's mistake.

"I'll be over in twenty minutes," he says.

I look at Frankie, who's struggling to stifle a yawn. It suddenly hits me that all I want to do right now is curl up in bed with her. "No, that's okay. There's really nothing you can do. They didn't take anything, just left kind of a mess."

"I'm good at cleaning up messes."

"No, that's all right, you get some sleep. I could use your help tomorrow morning. I think we need to have a look inside R.D.'s office."

"I think that's a real good idea. Is ten o'clock early enough?"

"That's just fine."

"Is Frankie okay?"

"Yeah, she's fine too."

I seal up the broken window with duct tape while Frankie straightens up the bedroom. I join her as soon as I'm done—after making sure every door and window in the house is locked. This definitely feels like closing the barn door after the horse is gone.

"Does it strike you as odd that Mitch spotted the burglar?" Frankie asks as I climb into bed beside her.

"No. Why?"

"I don't know. It seems like a big coincidence that he just happened to be taking out the garbage as the guy was leaving. Besides, Lydia's the one who takes out the garbage most of the time. She's always complaining that Mitch never does it."

"Are you suggesting Mitch is the one who did the break-in? I think you're stretching things a bit. Quite a bit."

"Maybe. But you know how firemen like to set fires just so they can put them out and get praised as heroes? He gave me that kind of feeling."

"This wasn't some contrived act of heroism. It was someone looking for the baseball cards. And we know our friend, the imaginary Larry Little, was responsible for it."

"What if Mitch turns out to be Larry Little?"

"He can't be."

"Why not?"

"Because Mitch was in my office today when Little called."

"But you said yourself it sounded like a different guy from the first one. You don't think it's curious that Mitch just happened to be there?"

"He stopped to see me. He does that sometimes. It probably occurred to him because he saw the item *your* friend ran in her column. And what about the car being a Fiero? Do you think he just happened to make that up? And if he is involved in this, that's the last make of car he'd invent."

Frankie yawns. "Oh, I don't know."

"You're just getting so twisted up that you're suspicious of everyone," I say.

"No, not everyone."

"Well almost everyone."

She smiles. "I haven't said a word about Pat and he has a Fiero."

I let out a groan of protest. "I think we have a pretty good idea whose car it was, Frankie."

"I was only kidding. But how do you think Beth Moony's car managed to cover so much territory in so short a period of time?"

"Mitch said the guy left two hours before we got home. That would have been around the time we were eating dinner."

"And just who do you suppose was driving it? Not Beth. Our impeccable witness Mitch said it was a big white fellow."

"I may have an idea about that," I say.

"And just what is that?"

"Remember I told you about the blonde I saw outside the hockey game with R.D.? I've got a sneaking suspicion it might have been Beth."

"You're not implying that that sweet young thing was two-timing your good friend Jerry?"

"It looks like R.D. was cheating on his girlfriend."

I slide my arm under Frankie's head and she turns over and presses against me, her hand resting on my chest. She feels warm and soothing, the nicest I've felt in what seems like weeks. We lay there like that in silence for a few minutes, until suddenly I feel her skin go cool.

"I only know one thing for sure," she says. "I don't care if you have to dump them down the sewer, I want those goddamn cards out of our hands tomorrow."

I could tell her the whole situation is out of our hands, that we're not controlling the cards as far as that part of it goes, but that would only lead to an argument and I dearly need to get some sleep.

"Tomorrow it'll all be over," I say. "That's a promise."

It's a promise I fully intend to keep, but when I finally doze off, I'm still not sure how I'll manage to do it.

22

Frankie again refuses to consider my counsel that she stay away from the house for the day. But I get her to agree to keep the doors locked and not let in anyone she doesn't know. Actually, that doesn't take any effort on my part. When I offer it as a suggestion, her response is, "What do you think I am—stupid?"

I go straight to my office, not even bothering to stop at Ronnie's for coffee. I've got a hunch to play, and I'm annoyed at myself for not thinking of it sooner. I may not know for sure who's trying to get the baseball cards from me, but it would help to find out where they came from.

It takes me a few minutes to remember the name of the sports shop where Tony Rio had bought his Mets cap a few days before he bought the farm. I should have written it down but I had a lot of things on my mind just then.

I remember that it's called Ivy League something-or-other, in Princeton. That's sufficient to get the number from directory assistance. This is the first time I've ever dealt with operators from coast to coast in such a short period of time. I may just be a hometown boy, but I really do like the Chicago recording voice the best. The one in New Jersey sounds like she moonlights as a toxic-waste hauler.

It's a man's voice that answers the phone at Irv's Ivy League Sports Collectibles. I get a visual picture of Senator Bill Bradley because he's the only guy I know of who went to Princeton, but he sounds more like a guy who *eats* toxic waste for breakfast. I don't know whether or not it's Irv.

"I have a rather strange question," I say.

"Go ahead, it won't be the first."

"I'm wondering if you're missing any baseball cards."

"What is this, some kind of a joke?" The guy's voice shoots up suddenly, and I assume his blood pressure is rising right along with it. "Because if it is, it ain't funny, asshole."

With that, he hangs up.

I think that answers my question. I can't imagine anyone being so sensitive about missing some baseball cards unless they are.

I hit redial. This time I try to get a few words in right off the bat. "Hello, my name's Phil Moony, I'm calling from Chicago. I just called and you hung—"

"What's with you, Moony? You think this is funny? How the fuck would you like it if some gorilla walked into your place, made you strip buck naked, and cleaned you out?"

I try to tell him there's a misunderstanding, but he's too busy screaming to listen.

"And if I find out you had anything to do with this, I'm going to go out there and burn your goddamn place to the ground! Do you hear me? I'll pound you so goddamn hard your whole family will hurt."

I wait for him to catch his breath before trying to respond. "I've got news for you, dickhead," I say. "Moony's dead." I slam down the phone. Let him marinate about that one for a while.

I glance at the clock when I hear the knock at the door. At first I think Pat's a few minutes early, but when I open the door I'm face-to-face-to-face with Vic Rosten and Shandra Washington.

"Good morning!" Rosten is beaming as he swaggers past me. "You don't look very happy to see us."

I guess the queasy feeling in my stomach must show on my face. I don't make any effort to cover. "I'm not."

"Yeah, most people aren't," he says, nodding knowingly. "We decided to take a chance and see if you were here. If we went to your house, your wife would probably call one of her bigshot newspaper friends and get some lies printed in the paper."

"How is your lovely wife, Mr. Moony?" Washington asks.

"She gets lovelier each day, Miss Washington. I'll tell her you asked. I'm sure she'll be pleased."

Washington lets out a little harumph, then turns when someone knocks on the door. This time it is Pat. He's still early and I'm glad he's here.

"Well, well, look what the cat dragged in." Rosten holds out his hand. "Hello, Commander. Long time no see."

Pat ignores the handshake. "What are you doing here?"

A widemouthed grin spreads over Rosten's face. "Me and my partner just stopped by to *harass* your friend here. At least I assume he's your friend."

"That's right. A good friend."

Rosten shakes his head disapprovingly. "Tsk, tsk. The company you keep, Patrick."

"You better not be giving him any trouble. I've still got some friends downtown."

"Yeah? Name one." Rosten's whole body heaves as he laughs. "Just doing our jobs, Pat. You know you can't believe anything you read in the paper." He nods toward his partner. "This is Shandra Washington."

Pat offers his hand. "Pat Ryan."

"This guy almost made commish a few years ago," Rosten says.

"I remember," she says as she takes Pat's hand. "It's an honor to meet you, sir."

"A pleasure. And it's Pat, not sir."

"That's right, bag the sir bit."

"Isn't this a little early for you to be working? I'd expect you to be shaking down some cross-eyed Greek for a free breakfast at this hour."

Rosten laughs again, looks at Washington and nods at Pat. "Guy's got a great sense of humor, don't he?"

She smiles, but you can tell her heart's not in it.

"I heard you were on the rent-a-cop circuit, Patrick. That's supposed to be very fulfilling work."

"Actually I've been working with gangs."

"Is that right?" Washington says. "What are you doing?"

Pat smiles. "I'm teaching them how to shoot straight. That way when they aim at your partner, they won't hit any innocent bystanders."

The smile vanishes from Rosten's face. "That ain't funny."

Pat shrugs. "So, have you got anything to ask him, or are you just killing time until lunch?"

"Oh, I'd say a little of both." Rosten tilts his head back and sizes me up, providing me with a view up his nostrils. "We found out this Tony Rio who turned up cold in the Milshire Hotel got out of the slam in New Jersey a week ago. He matches the description of a guy who knocked over a baseball card shop out there. Remember that suitcase I told you about, that the desk clerk said Rio was carrying? We figure maybe it wasn't filled with dope, after all. It might've been filled with baseball cards. That's pretty funny, isn't it? That somebody would kill someone over fucking baseball cards?" He smiles. "But that's not why we're here to see you. We're here to see you about bourbon."

He pauses for effect. If the effect is to make me nervous, it's working quite nicely.

"Jim Beam bourbon, as a matter of fact. Is that your brand, Phil?"

I try to take a deep breath without opening my mouth. It ain't easy. While making the attempt, I manage to get out an answer. "Sometimes." It's barely audible.

"Yeah, I thought so. In fact, I know so. We traced a receipt we found in the bag to the liquor store around the corner."

"Someone left the receipt right in the bag for you to find, is that right, Vic? Well you must be dealing with a real crafty son of a bitch, huh?"

"That don't mean it couldn't be him, do it?" Rosten chortles, gestures at me and shoots a glance at his partner at the same time. She's wearing one of those "*Boy would I like to shoot this honky asshole*" sulks on her face.

Pat shakes his head. "Sounds like an Area Five Special. Oh I'm sorry, I guess that doesn't go on there anymore, not since they brought you in to straighten things out."

"What the fuck do you know?"

"You don't by any chance still have the communal evidence bag over in Five, do you?"

"We got computers now, Pat. Our methods have gotten a lot more modern since you left."

"What, do you keep track of your payoffs on spread sheets? Come on, hurry up, ask your questions."

"I will. Now that you've given me back the floor." Rosten looks at me. "The guy at the liquor store tells me *you* bought a pint of Beam three days ago. Is that right?"

"I don't remember."

"You don't remember!"

"I buy booze there all the time. I don't keep track of the dates."

Rosten lights a cigarette. "Well evidently he does. And he's pretty sure it was three days ago. Now the curious thing is, that's the same brand we found in Rio's hotel room. Same brand, same size. Only the stuff he drank had cyanide in it. You can't buy it that way at the store. If that's how you want it, you got to mix it yourself."

"Get to the goddamn point," Pat says.

"Oh yeah, the point. Well, we were feeling kind of thirsty so we thought we'd drop in and see if Moony would pour us a drink."

"It's a little early in the day for me," I say.

"That's what she said." Rosten chuckles as he scans the shelves. "Boy, I don't see any booze. I guess you must keep it in the desk, huh?"

I shake my head as we get into a stare-down.

"Well then, where is it?"

"I don't have any."

"You mean to say you drank it all? Man, you must've been thirsty."

"It was only a pint. I could've knocked that off between here and the liquor store."

He smiles. "Yeah, I guess so. Especially if you had Pat helping you."

"Did you find any prints on the goddamn bottle or not?" Pat asks.

"Good question." He turns slowly to face Pat. "A couple."

"Were any of them his?"

"*Very* good question." Rosten grins. "I see you haven't lost your stuff, Pat."

I feel my heart moving up into my throat and my stomach sliding toward my ankles.

"Well, what's the fucking answer?" Pat demands.

"No."

I try not to let out a sigh of relief as my internal organs return to their natural positions.

"Then why the fuck are you bothering him about it?"

"We've got to check out every lead, Pat. You know that. And of course you also know that just because his prints aren't on the bottle don't mean he didn't do it." He sighs heavily. "I'd feel a whole lot better if you still had that bottle in your office here, Phil."

"Well I don't!" Now that I know I'm in the clear, I feel free to go on the offensive. "And if you were checking out leads instead of fucking with my head, you might learn that the other guy named Phil Moony that I told you about owns a baseball card shop up in Morton Grove."

"Yeah, yeah, we know that," Rosten says. "There's only one problem. That Phil Moony died of a heart attack earlier this week. Which means he ain't saying much. And besides, you're more fun to talk to anyway."

"Are you done having your fun?" Pat asks.

"Yeah, I suppose." Rosten takes two steps toward the door,

then stops. "Oh, just one more thing. That phone call to nine-one-one that tipped us off about Rio? It was placed from the phone booth outside this building."

He waits for my reaction but I don't give him one.

"Now I suppose you don't know anything about that, do you?"

I hold out my hands, palms up. "Sorry I can't help you."

"Yeah, I thought so. You were probably busy drinking all that bourbon." He looks at his watch. "Well, partner, it looks like it's almost getting to be that time."

"Four square meals a day whether you need them or not. Right, Vic?" Pat says.

"That's right."

"Try the Orbit up Milwaukee past Diversey," I say.

"Do you believe this guy?" Rosten hooks his thumb at me while speaking to Washington. "He thinks he can tell *me* about Polish food."

She almost gives me a smile. "He practically lives there."

That's the best news I've heard all day. The only reason I suggested it was because the one time I ate there I had the runs for a week.

Rosten extends his hand. "Patrick, always a pleasure." This time Pat takes it, but he doesn't return the greeting. While he and Washington say good-bye, Rosten turns to me for the last word.

"We'll be back, Moony."

"I'll buy a quart next time so there'll be something left."

Over a cup of coffee I brief Pat on all that's happened since we saw each other yesterday. When it comes to sorting and sifting through data, he's got the mind of a computer, but by the time I finish he says he feels a migraine coming on.

"Here's what it sounds like it comes down to," he says, pacing the room and working his fingers like an abacus. "Rio steals the cards from the shop in New Jersey. In all likelihood he's working for Moony, who knows the shop owner out there. From what you said, it sounds like they had a personal feud going. But someone close to Moony gets wind of the scheme and decides to cash in. Moony's wife perhaps, or maybe his son. Or maybe it's his daughter and her boyfriend—*your* landlord. But you think the daughter may also be involved with R.D., so that adds another wrinkle to it. In any case we know that the wife has to be in on it, because she pretends to believe Larry Little is still alive when she's got to know he died almost twenty years ago."

"Unless she's led a very sheltered existence."

"From the way you describe her, she hasn't." Pat pauses to blow his nose. He's one of the last of the breed that carries a bandana for a handkerchief. "Now whoever her partner is, he must know something about your background. I doubt you were chosen merely because you had the same name, though that obviously helped. When Rio called you, he thought he was talking to the other Phil Moony, right?"

I shake my head. "When Rio called me, he was already dead.

The guy who called was pretending to be Rio so he could get me over to the hotel room."

"That's right. You're right, I'm wrong. But my point is that whoever set you up to be their courier knew a few things about you. He knew you worked here, which is why he signed Rio in at the Milshire. He knew it was just around the corner, so it wouldn't be much effort for you to get over there. It also wouldn't take long for you to get back. He could call you from the pay phone downstairs, watch you leave, then be waiting here when you returned. Knock you over the head, snatch the suitcase, and *adios.*"

"The thing I don't understand is how he could be sure I'd take the briefcase."

"That's where knowing your background comes in. A guy who's been in trouble with the cops doesn't leave a package with his name and address on it lying next to a stiff in a hotel room. Especially when the guy's been in trouble for drugs and the package looks like it's got drugs in it. The guy must have told Rio to slap that label on it. Even if he forgets, even if you for some reason decide to leave the package there, what has he lost? A few minutes of his time. Because if that happened, he could decide whether or not to go fetch it himself."

Pat smiles. "When you think about it, it's really a brilliant little plan. The guy that thought it up it must be a genius. You know any?"

"If I do, I'm not aware of that part of their personality." I get up from my chair. "But I really don't know very much about R.D. Do you have your burglar's tools with you?"

Pat pulls a screwdriver out of his jacket pocket as he stands up.

"You can pick a lock with *that?*"

"You're the only tenant on this floor besides R.D., right? So screw the lock. We'll take the goddamn door right off its hinges."

That turns out to be easier said than done. The hinges have been on the door since the Cubs last won a pennant, and they've had more coats of paint than Wrigley Field. It takes at least ten minutes to pry the top bolt off. The bottom one is halfway up the sleeve when we hear footsteps at the top of the stairs around the bend.

"Are you expecting anyone?" Pat whispers.

"No. But I've had a lot of unannounced visitors lately. It also could be Jerry, the landlord."

Whoever it is, the steps are coming in our direction. I leave R.D.'s bundle of mail on the floor and we stumble to the end of the hall, around the corner to the back of the building. We listen from there as the footsteps quicken, then stop abruptly outside R.D.'s office.

"What the fuck?" I hear a familiar voice say.

"Just the guy we want to talk to," I say to Pat, tugging at his sleeve as I start back around the corner. "Hello, R.D.," I call to the figure in the red Blackhawks jacket staring dumbfounded at the door.

I half expect him to take off running, but he doesn't. Instead he wheels to face me.

"Hey, Phil, what's happening?" He gestures at the door. "Somebody tried to break into my office."

"It was us," I say as Pat moves up beside me.

"What?"

"Remember, you wanted me to drop off your mail?" I say as I walk toward him.

"Yeah but . . . I gave you a key. What did you do, lose it?"

"No, R.D., I didn't lose it. I've still got it." I pull the set of keys he gave me out of my pocket. "Only it doesn't work."

"Bullshit, let me see it." He takes the keys from my hand and tries one in the lock. It doesn't work. He tries another and it doesn't work either. "That's funny," he says.

"Don't tell me you're surprised."

"What?"

"Listen, R.D., why don't you cut out the naive act. You've got a lot of explaining to do and I don't have a whole lot of patience today."

"Me! You're the guy that tried to yank the door off."

"That's nothing compared to the grief you've been causing me."

"Hey man, I don't know what you're talking about." His anger melts into anxiety as Pat glowers at him. Pat's getting up there in years, but he's still an intimidating presence. "Who's this dude?"

"I'm a friend of his," Pat says. "And I'm not a dude."

"You're the guy that came by my place with him, aren't you?"

"Yeah, that's right."

"Jenny told me about that," he says to me. "Man, why did you do that? I'm in hot water up to my eyeballs with her on account of you. You told her you saw me at the hockey game."

"I did. *After* you told me you were going to New York."

"Yeah, I know. But that fell through."

"So where've you been the last couple of days? I've been looking all over for you."

"Why?"

"Why don't you just tell us where you've been," Pat says.

"What is this? Are you a cop or something?"

"Or something," Pat says.

"What about you?" I ask. "Are you a cop?"

"Are you kidding? Hell no. I hate cops."

There's a long pause as R.D. stares incredulously at us, then realizes he's probably insulted Pat, then suddenly looks away. Either he's a very good actor or he doesn't have a clue. Whichever it is, I still want some answers.

"Okay, here's what happened," he says. "My client canceled my trip to New York at the last minute. So I was really feeling bummed. I was looking forward to going to the Apple. Things with Jenny haven't been going so hot and I really could've used the break. But then I end up having to stay here. On top of that I gave my hockey tickets to you."

"You didn't give them to me, you sold them to me."

"Same difference." He frowns. "Don't worry, it won't happen again."

"Who's your client, by the way?" Pat asks.

"Sports Channel America. I did their logo, they wanted me to do some other stuff." He glances at his office as if he's considering whether to move inside. "So anyway I call this old girlfriend of mine who works for an ad agency. They've got the Bud account and they can always get tickets. It turns out she just busted up with her boyfriend. She wants to go to the game with me and it sounds like she wouldn't mind doing a little more than that, if you know what I mean." He grins. "So I figure this is my chance to get a little vacation from Jenny after all. She thinks I'm going to the Apple for a couple days, I'll just hang out with my old girlfriend." He shrugs. "And that's it."

"What's the girl's name?" Pat asks. "Is it Beth?"

"No, Marlese. You want her phone number?"

Pat and I exchange looks. "I think he could be telling the truth," he says.

"Of course I'm telling the truth. What's with you guys, anyway?"

"What were you doing in my office on Tuesday?"

"What, you mean when I came to give you the tickets?"

"No, I mean after that, around lunch hour."

"I don't know what you're talking about."

"There was a guy in my office on Tuesday. I saw him through the window. He was about your size. And he had on a Blackhawks jacket, just like you wear."

"Well it sure the fuck wasn't me. How the hell would I get into your office?"

"With this." I reach out and take the keys out of his hand. "This doesn't open your office, it opens mine."

"That's crazy."

"You want to see?" I start down the hall, with Pat and R.D. trailing. He's carrying his mail and a slack-jawed expression that conveys the bewilderment of a lost dog. I put the key in my lock and turn it. "There, what do you think of that?"

R.D. shakes his head and his long hair intensifies the shaggy-dog look. "I don't know what to think, man. That's just weird. Really weird."

"So you don't have any explanation for why you have a key to his office," Pat says.

"No. You'd have to ask Jerry. He gave me two sets of keys when I moved in. I gave the extra set to you."

I take the key off the ring and slip it in my pocket, then give the ring with the other two keys back to R.D. "Well, I guess I'll have to talk to Jerry."

"Yeah, you do that. Now, do you mind telling me what this is all about?"

"Sorry, I can't do that."

He gives Pat a hateful look. "Am I free to go now?"

Pat puffs up his cheeks and blows out air as he looks to me for an answer. All I can do is shrug. I don't see any point in asking R.D. any more questions, like whether he collects baseball cards or what kind of car he drives.

"Sure, you can go," Pat says.

R.D. strides off, making a show of shaking his head and gushing big sighs of annoyance. When he gets about ten yards down the hall, he turns and calls, "Hey, what about my door?"

"What about it?" Pat says.

"Aren't you going to put it back on?"

Pat walks toward him, holding the bolt in his hand. "A big strong cop-hating dude like you? I think you can handle it."

Pat looks at his watch. "You're supposed to meet this Little guy at what time, three o'clock?" We're having lunch in the Mexican joint across from the Turkey.

"Yeah, if he shows up."

"What makes you think he won't show up?"

"Because he's been dead for twenty years, remember?"

Pat chuckles and takes a swig of Carta Blanca. "Would you be terribly disappointed if I didn't make it?"

"He said he wanted me to come alone."

"Yeah I know, but I was figuring on keeping an eye on things from up the street in my car."

"You sure that's a good idea?"

"I'm not sure I can even do it. My sister Cathy called this morning and reminded me we're supposed to go to Wisconsin and see my uncle Jack. He's my old man's brother, lives in a nursing home outside Madison. He's going in for surgery tomorrow and they're not sure he's going to make it. I'd completely forgotten about it until she called. She's all pissed off at me because I told her I couldn't go. But now, well, I'm starting to have second thoughts."

I reach into my pocket for a quarter and toss it on the table. "You call her up right now and tell her you're going."

"I don't know. I feel bad leaving you in the lurch."

"Bullshit. You feel bad missing out on all this cops and robbers stuff. It's in your blood and this whole thing's got it flowing again."

He plays with the quarter, thinking things over. "You sure you wouldn't mind?"

I'd be lying if I said I wasn't disappointed not having Pat around in case I need help. But it wasn't him who got me into this mess, it was me.

"It's not a question of minding," I say. "It's a question of doing what's right."

He nods slowly as he picks up the quarter and closes his hand over it. Suddenly he gets animated, pointing his finger at me.

"Okay, but here's what I want you to do: When you go to meet this guy today, don't bring the cards with you. He's not going to do anything to you until he has his grubby little hands on the cards. You tell him your price, and make sure he gives you something up front today. Do you know how much you're going to ask for?"

I shake my head. "At this point, Pat, I don't care. I just want to get rid of the damn things. Frankie gave me an ultimatum on that last night."

"Well, you're a fool if you don't hold him up for at least a few grand. This guy's caused you a lot of trouble. He should pay."

I feel my eyes widen in amazement and I can tell Pat notices, because he asks me what's wrong.

"Nothing. I'm just surprised to hear you saying this. You're not talking like the squeaky-clean cop I once knew."

"Yeah well, I'm not a cop anymore. And besides, this is different. You're not using your position to profit off people. You were put in this position without any choice. Once you unload the cards, you can tip off the cops, let them know your suspicions about Moony's wife and your landlord and anyone else you think might be involved. But not until *after* you've gotten rid of the cards."

I nod. I haven't really thought this thing all the way through. I'm still playing it by ear.

"So what I want you to do is set up an exchange for tomorrow night. I'll go along with you."

"How are you going to get back so soon? Your uncle's only going in for surgery tomorrow?"

"Don't worry, I'll get back. Cathy will stay up there for a couple of days. We've been through this drill three times before with Uncle Jack. They cut on the guy once a year. Far as I'm concerned, the son of a bitch is going to outlive all of us."

"Do you know a place to do the exchange?"

"You kidding? I know a million of them."

"All we need is one."

He stands up and waves the quarter. "Let me call Cathy. I'll tell you when I get back."

I get the check and pay it while Pat's calling his sister. When he returns his round face is beaming like a neon basketball. "You got me back in the goods with her again." He glances at the table and sees the tip I've put down. He starts for his wallet, but I put out my hand.

"This one's mine. I recently got an unexpected windfall from a mysterious benefactor."

He snorts. "You call that a windfall? For guys in vice, that's a slow day."

I start to get up, but he signals for me to remain seated. "Have you got a pen? Write this down."

I sit poised, using the back of the personalized stationery Mitch left on our door last night. It ended up in the back pocket of my jeans.

"You know where St. Pascal's church is, on Irving Park Road?"

"Sure, that's the place where the mob accosted Mayor Harold when he went to Sunday mass during the first election campaign."

"Yeah, that's right, fine group of people. They've got ten Dumpsters in the alley in back. Cleanest Dumpsters in the city. The only thing they use them for is Bingo on Thursday nights, and the garbagemen come on Friday morning. Tell your guy to drop the money in the Dumpster farthest to the west at nine-thirty tomorrow night. Then walk two blocks east to the Patio theater. Go to the phone booth in the lobby. Wait by the phone booth and you'll call within ten minutes and tell him where to pick up the cards."

"And where's that?"

"In the same Dumpster. You'll leave the cards when you pick up the money."

"What if somebody's watching?"

He shrugs. "If somebody's watching, the whole deal's off. Be sure to tell him that."

I must look a little skeptical. I'm certainly feeling that way.

"Listen, that's only if you want to hold them up for money. You could just as easily pull a fistful of cards off the top for yourself and just drop the rest and be done with it. How are they going to know which cards are supposed to be there?"

"I think I like that way of doing things better."

"Suit yourself. But whatever you do, don't tell him where the cards are going to be. Make him go to a phone and wait for your call. That way you don't have someone waiting in the alley for you with a .38."

"You wouldn't happen to know the number on that phone in the theater, would you?"

Pat grins. "Hey, I'm good, but I'm not that good."

Outside the restaurant we shake hands. "Be careful," Pat says. "Don't forget to take along that toy I gave you. And whatever you do, don't drink anything with cyanide in it."

I return to the office and call Jerry Gabriel. I don't know what I'm going to say when he answers, but it doesn't matter because I get his machine. I don't bother to leave a message.

I call Frankie and get the news that there's no news. Evidently, our friends have gotten tired of breaking into our house. The only thing worrying her is my meeting with Larry Little. I tell her nothing's going to happen in broad daylight or an empty bar. She begs me to be careful and I tell her I'll be home in time for dinner.

"Oh no," she says. "We're going out for dinner." She's trying hard to be cheerful, but I can tell her patience is wearing thin.

There's no point in hanging around the office, so I head for the Irish Wolfhound early. I get there a little after two-thirty. As I expected, the place is empty.

It's a tiny joint, a dozen stools along the bar and a pair of tables on either side of the jukebox, which has every song the Clancy Brothers ever did, and not much more. I've only been here a few times, but I've taken a healthy liking to the place. One reason is the owner, an Irish woman in her forties who's tall enough to play in the pros if she could only sink a jump shot. I ask her name every time I come in, and every time I come back I've forgotten it. As I order a Harp, I find out it's Rita.

Another reason I like the place is it's quiet. The patrons tend to be oldsters who come by themselves. They rarely make any noise, except when they put their heads on the bar and start to snore like AWOL sailors. This seems to be a nightly ritual. The thing I like most about the place is the dogs. There are two of them. One's an Irish wolfhound named Shannon. He spends most of his time in the back room, wandering out to the bar only when customers enter and exit, serving the dual function of low-budget bouncer and greeter. The other is an ancient cocker spaniel who likes nothing better than to perch on a stool with his paws on the bar and sip Guinness from a Styrofoam cup. His name is Conroy. The first night I went into the place, Conroy and I were the only guys drinking. Everyone else was asleep.

I take the first seat at the bar, which affords a view out the front window. Because the door swings inward, it also enables me to see people who enter before they see me. But no one enters. Not for the first half hour, which passes slower than Easter mass. I pass the time nursing my Harp and playing the Pogues on the jukebox to drown out "Donahue" on the black-and-white TV at the other end of the bar. On my second round I try to buy a Guinness for Conroy, but Rita says he's on a strict diet that prohibits alcohol before five P.M. I buy myself a pack of Camels instead.

By the time three-fifteen rolls around, I'm practically ready for the asylum. I've forsaken the stool because I can't sit still. I take out my wallet and empty my pockets, using the opportunity to reduce the paper accumulation of the last few days. Amidst the clutter of bank withdrawal slips, liquor store receipts, stamps and ticket stubs, I come upon a scrap of paper with a name on it. It takes a few moments to decipher my handwriting and see that the name is Karl Mitchell, the guy Pat told me was the manager of the Purple Haze. As I stare at the name long and hard, it occurs to me that of the four people associated with the club, Mitchell is the only one my phantom phone caller hasn't mentioned. He's impersonated Larry Little, Tony Rio and the other Phil Moony, but he hasn't said a peep about Karl Mitchell.

"This is the fucking guy," I say aloud. Suddenly I feel very dumb for not making the connection sooner. I wonder why Pat didn't focus in on it.

"Excuse me?" Rita says.

I wave her away. "Nothing. I was just talking to myself."

She grins. "Better watch out, that's the first stage of senility." She clears away the crumpled bits of paper that I've piled next to the ashtray.

I toss the scrap with Mitchell's name on the Save pile, on top of the sheet with Pat's instructions for setting up the exchange. I take two steps to the pay phone and punch in the number to my office to check the messages on my machine. The last one is from Frankie from three days ago, back when my life was practically worry-free. I call her, thinking the guy may have tried to reach me at home. I don't even get Frankie, just her voice on our answering machine.

That makes me nervous. She didn't say anything about going out. Not that I expect her to check in with me every time she leaves the house, but today I think she would have said something.

I talk into the machine, hoping she's screening her calls. She does that sometimes, but this isn't one of them. I babble on until I hear the beep, a full minute of meandering monologue. I don't have any idea what I've just said.

I step back to the bar and look up at the clock. It's three-thirty. I've got that sinking feeling I've been stood up. I tell myself Frankie probably just ran out to the drugstore to get cigarettes. I light one of my own and resolve to stick it out until it's finished.

I glance down at the papers in front of me. I stare at the name Karl Mitchell, positioned under the heading that says, *From the Desk of . . .*

"I don't fucking believe it. Frankie was right."

Rita strolls toward me and shoots me a wink. "You're doing it again."

I ask her for another Harp. I should lay off the beer so I've got my wits about me, but I feel like nothing short of a shot would do anything to soothe my shattered nerves. I can't possibly keep my wits when my nerves are shattered. I order a shot of Jameson's.

Rita's halfway down the bar when the phone rings. She picks it up, listens for a moment, then looks at me. "Are you Moony?"

I scamper along the bar to take it as she stretches the cord as far as it will reach. As I put it to my ear and hear the all-too-familiar voice, I don't have any trouble getting a mental picture of my caller. In one of those bizarre linkages that boggle the mind, I even get a whiff of bug spray.

"This is Larry Little."

I've got an urge to tell him I know who he is, but I suppress that, realizing it gives me the upper hand. Instead I try to maintain my usual smartass posture. "You died twenty years ago," I say.

He laughs. "That's right, I forgot."

"Where are you? I've been waiting. Your beer's getting warm."

"I don't like the looks of the place. I'm changing the meeting spot."

"You seem to be forgetting something: I'm holding the cards."

"Not anymore you're not. I've got the ace."

"What's that supposed to mean?" I close my eyes as I say it. I already know the answer to the question.

"Your wife, the bitch of spades."

"Bullshit."

"I'm afraid not, Phil. You want me to prove it?"

I don't answer. I can't answer. My tongue is caught motionless between rage and fear.

"Tell you what you do," he says. "You hang up and stay by the phone. I'll have her call you."

"You fucking asshole, if anything happens to her . . ."

"Don't get hysterical, Phil. Just do what I tell you and the bitch will be just fine. Now hang up like a good little boy and wait for the call."

Rita takes the phone from me without a word. She doesn't let on that I've got higher ratings than "Donahue" in her book, but I know she knows something's up. In a shaky voice, I manage to tell her I'm expecting a call back.

I down the shot that she's put in front of me, then move back down the bar to retrieve my beer. From watching the clock I can see that it takes only three minutes for the phone to ring. They're the longest three minutes of my life.

"Hello Phil." Frankie's voice sounds distant and frail.

"Are you all right?"

"Fine, all things considered."

"Where are you?"

"In a van. I don't know where exactly. I've got a blindfold on. A guy broke into the house and—"

"Okay, that's enough," a loud voice says. I recognize the nasal tone of the caller who did the bad imitation of Larry Little when the real Little impersonator was in my office yesterday.

"I love you, Phil."

The car phone must be a hands-free model because Frankie's voice still comes through at the same volume. That means her captor can hear every word I say.

"I love you too, Frankie." I say it with as much feeling as I ever have, but I barely muscle it out past the lump in my throat.

He lets out a short laugh. "Ah, ain't that sweet. If you love her, you'll do exactly as you're told. Now wait for the call back. That'll have your instructions."

"Please don't hurt her."

"Nobody's going to get hurt, Moony, unless you fuck up. Remember that."

I hold out the handset for Rita. "One more," I say.

"Beer or Jameson's."

I shake my head. "Phone call."

This time it takes less than a minute. Rita passes the phone with one hand and puts a shot down in front of me with the other. "This one's on me," she whispers.

I try to nod appreciatively, but it's not easy while listening to the scumbag who's kidnapped my wife.

"Okay, asshole, listen carefully. It's four o'clock now. You've got exactly one hour. Here's what you do. Put the cards in a green trashbag. Tie a knot in the top of it, don't use one of those fucking twist ties. Get on the Edens and go north to Winnetka. Get off at the Willow Road exit, going east. Take Willow half a mile, past the first stoplight. On your right, you'll see the town dump. Turn in the driveway and go behind the building. You'll see a row of recycling bins. We're going to do some recycling. You're a friend of the earth, aren't you, Phil?"

I don't bother to answer.

"Get out of the car, drop the trashbag into the bin for plastic. Not newspapers, not glass, not aluminum, *plastic*. Then get back in your car and drive the fuck away. That's all there is to it. Don't wait around and don't bring your cop friend with you. Can you remember all that? Do you want me to repeat it?"

"No, I've got it. What about my wife?"

"Your wife's going to be just fine, as long as you follow instructions. If you fuck up, don't expect to see her ever again."

"I won't fuck up. Just tell me where I can find her."

"As soon as I get the cards, she'll be let go. She'll be dropped off right at your door. Depending on traffic, she'll probably get there before you do. Maybe she'll even have supper waiting for you."

I don't say anything.

"Well, you better get going. You only got an hour."

I drop the phone on the bar, not even waiting for Rita to get control of it. I'm at the door when she calls out.

"You forgot your change." She waves a five-dollar bill.

I wave my hand. "Give Conroy the night of his life."

I head straight home. I don't have any choice but to take Irving Park. But Irving Park is a moat. The whole northwest side is a clutter of construction gravesites, as a matter of fact. The Kennedy is a war zone for three years, and they've only now decided to refurbish some alternate routes. For this we're supposed to thank Congressman Dan Rostenkowski, powerful chairman of the House Ways and Means Committee.

I play checkers on the side streets, probably putting some school children in jeopardy, but I manage to make it home in ten minutes. Winnetka at this hour is a twenty-minute drive. In fifteen minutes it will be a half-hour drive. I park a block south, on the dead-end service road that rims the expressway. I walk up the alley that runs behind the east side of our street, Hamlin. This puts two houses, two garages and two backyards in the sightline from Mitch's house to me. I cut over near the north end of our block, at the second house in from the corner. This dumps me out right across from the Miglins'. Their house sits directly behind Mitch's. I consider going next door to check our house for clues about where Frankie is, but at this point I think I'm better off following directions.

Using the shrubs along the north side of the Miglins' house for cover, I have no trouble darting to the garage. If Mitch is looking out the window, I'm sure he'd be watching our house.

The first sign of trouble I encounter is the padlock. As I take it in my hand to push the key into the lock, it slides open. I can't believe I left it unlocked, but I can't for certain remember locking it.

As I take my first step inside and begin to grope in the darkness, I lose my balance and stumble forward. Plunging into blackness, I feel the terror of falling ten stories. I try to stifle the scream curling up in my throat, but I'm not sure if I do. My hands shoot out instinctively to break my fall. It ends an instant later when my knees collide with the floor. It's a soft landing, definitely not concrete. But my arms are jolted from the impact and I get a major fucking league case of pins and needles.

I collapse to the floor, flapping like a speeding turtle. I stay that way for a few moments, waiting for my eyes to adjust. Beneath me I can feel a bed of magazines. As the room lightens I can see they're mostly *National Geographics*, charbroiled from the fire. Someone moved them to the doorway.

I scramble toward the bag of cards on hands and knees. My heart is pounding so madly that my chest is hitting the floor. There are no more obstacles in my path. But of course there wouldn't be. When I reach my secret hiding place, I already know the path is a dead end. But I grope frantically anyway, clearing debris and cobwebs with my arms in an attempt to pound the shit out of utter futility.

Mickey Mantle, Ted Williams, Roberto Clemente, Babe Ruth—they're all gone. They're all fucking gone.

I feel myself start to cry. As I listen to my sobs echoing off the walls, I realize what I sound like. The thought makes me cry harder. I sound just like a little kid who's lost all his baseball cards.

26

The biggest regret Mitch is ever going to have is that he showed me where he keeps the key to the side door of his garage. That's what I'm thinking as I slide the key back into the crevice between his rotting wooden window and his ancient asbestos siding.

I've got no doubt that Mitch has been orchestrating this whole miserable charade from the beginning. Frankie would not have let anyone she didn't know into the house. There's a remote chance someone broke in while she was out, but I'm almost certain she didn't go out. The meeting at the Irish Wolfhound was all a sham to make sure I wasn't home. If I wasn't so overwhelmed with terror about something happening to Frankie, I'd be wallowing in self-contempt for letting myself be outwitted by Mitch Fucking Michaels.

There'll be plenty of time for self-loathing later. Right now I have to get something done the way I've always gotten things done—by not following directions.

To get to Winnetka by five o'clock, Mitch should be leaving in fifteen minutes. That's *if* he's home. *And* if he's the one who's picking up the cards. He's got one partner for sure. That's the guy who's got Frankie. I'm assuming he doesn't have another.

Big ifs, big assumption. I figure I can afford to stay ten minutes.

There are two cars in the garage: the Corvette and the Taurus. That's a good sign. Usually Lydia's Oldsmobile is parked here, but Friday is her day to go to the health club. Don't ask me how

I know that, I just do. This is the sort of thing you learn when you eat dinner at their house. There's a chance Mitch could be out in the van, but I'm assuming that's where his partner is holding Frankie. That's not a huge assumption, but every one is big right now. I figure they both had to be in the neighborhood recently, when Frankie was kidnapped. With Lydia gone, Mitch most likely would set up his base of operations at home. That would afford him a view of our house, to see if I came home.

I'm 99 percent sure the cocksucker didn't see me.

I take out my toy, as Pat calls it, and stand in the corner behind the side door. There's a brown shopping bag from Cub Foods pushed under the work table. Through the crack in the top, the cap to a bottle is visible. Quietly, I unfold the top of the bag. There are four bottles inside. Three of them are familiar. Until two days ago, they formed the Executive Lounge at Moony Enterprises. One of the bottles is a pint of Jim Beam. That provides me with the first sigh of relief I've had in a while. This isn't the bottle that ended up in Tony Rio's hotel room.

It's the fourth bottle that really interests me. It's plastic and has a much sterner warning label than the surgeon general's wimpy homily—a skull and crossbones. Mitch has held on to his cyanide. Maybe he intends to use it on someone. My guess would be Lydia, but that's just personal preference.

I carry the bag to the Corvette and put it on the floor on the passenger side. I don't need the booze, but I don't want to leave anything with my fingerprints on it in Mitch's garage. As far as the cyanide goes, I have a feeling there might be a use for it.

I don't hear the footsteps until he gets right outside the door. That still gives me time to collect myself while he fiddles with the lock. I wait until the door closes behind him before making my presence known. I do that by forming my forearms into a cross-bar and driving them into the back of his neck. He grunts as he lurches forward, then grunts again as he slams shoulder-first into the side of the Taurus. The second grunt sounds like he's in some pain. I take two steps over and plant my foot in the middle of his back. I dig in until I feel his vertebrae through the sole of my sneaker. He twists his head pathetically in an effort to see me. He's gasping for air and groaning at the same time. If it weren't for having to find Frankie, I believe I'd stomp this guy to death right now.

"Hello, Larry," I say quietly, pressing deeper with my foot, then dropping onto his lower back with my other knee.

"Ah fuck."

I put the gun under his ear, jamming the metal against his cranium. "Dickhead, when I get through with you, you're going to wish you did die twenty years ago."

"Listen, Phil, we can work something out." He tries to turn but I push his head back against the floor.

"You bet we can work something out, Mitch. But it's going to be on my terms. Are you packing a heater?"

"No."

Keeping the gun pressed to his head with my right hand, I frisk him with my left. Then I back off and get to my feet. "Now stand up real slowly and put your hands in the air."

He obeys to the letter, except that he's so wobbly he has to lean on the car for support. Once he steadies himself, he turns and raises his hands. He sneers when he sees the gun in my hand. "You think you could kill me with that peashooter?"

I give him a love tap across the face with it, and he topples back against the car. "There's only room for one smart-ass here, Mitch, and that's me. Understand?"

He nods as he holds his hands to his nose. It's bleeding.

"And for your information, I've got no intention of killing you. I'll probably just shoot off your pecker with the first shot and drill a new asshole through the left hemisphere of your cerebral cortex with the other." I smile. "That way, you won't be able to answer back when Lydia talks to you."

"Come on, Phil, cut the shit. I'll give you ten thousand for the cards and we'll let Frankie go right away."

"Damn right you'll let Frankie go right away." I motion with the gun. "Get on the phone to your partner and tell him to release her. In front of our house. If she has to walk more than fifty feet, I start shooting."

"What about the cards?"

"Fuck the cards. Make the call now or you'll be doing it without your dick." I aim the gun at his crotch for emphasis.

"All right, all right, take it easy." He starts to open the door to the Taurus.

"No, we're taking the 'Vette."

He shrugs. "Whatever you say."

I follow three steps behind him, keeping the gun trained on his back. I've got forty pounds and four inches on the guy, so I probably don't need it. But I'm not taking any chances. When we get to the car, I tell him to open the secret compartment where he keeps his .38. "By the way," I say, "that was awfully white of you to mention that little detail after you broke into our house last night."

He turns to face me. "I didn't break into your house last night."

"Bullshit."

"No it's not. I did it the first night, but last night that was someone else."

"Any idea who?"

"No. But it wasn't me."

"What about your partner?"

He shakes his head. "Nope. Not without me knowing."

"Then we have ourselves another little mystery, don't we?" As I complete the thought, I suddenly realize what the solution to the mystery is. "Yeah, now that I think about it, I guess it couldn't have been you. You wouldn't have been so considerate."

"What are you talking about? I'm the one that left you five hundred bucks. Just like I promised."

"Oh, that's right. I guess you really are a thoughtful guy. By the way, who is your partner?"

"You mean you haven't figured that out?"

"I've got a pretty good idea. In addition to Betty Moony, I mean."

"What does Betty have to do with this?"

"Plenty, obviously. Last night, at her husband's wake, she acted like she didn't know Larry Little's been dead twenty years. You told her to say that. Which was a major fuckup, pal. Or maybe it was your partner who gave her that advice. He's the one I told I was going to be at the wake." I smile. "Who fucked up, Mitch? You or Jerry?"

"Who?"

"Jerry Gabriel."

"Who's that?"

"Oh come on, Mitch, be serious."

"I am serious."

"Beth Moony's boyfriend? He's not in this with you?"

"You mean Mr. Turtleneck? He's not her boyfriend. He's just the guy she's fucking this month. What the fuck makes you think he's involved?"

"Because he's the landlord of my building on Kedzie."

"You're kidding."

"No, I'm not. You mean to say you didn't know that? Come on, get real."

"I'm telling the truth."

"Bullshit. How'd you get into my office? Jerry gave you the key, didn't he?"

"Hell no. I've had your keys for months." He grins. "You know that spare set you keep down in your basement? I got news for you—they ain't there anymore. Hell, I could steal your car if I wanted to. Not that I'd ever want to. But if you think I'd cover for that jerk, you're crazy. I only met him once, and that was by accident. Betty and me have been pretty discreet." He chuckles. "All these years."

"How long?"

He grins. "Real long."

"If you and Betty have been involved for so long, why'd you wait until now to get rid of Moony?"

"Because of the cards. Between his insurance and the cards, me and Betty are set for life."

"Not anymore you aren't."

"Ah come on, Phil. We can still work something out."

I motion with the gun. "Why don't you start working that compartment open."

It only takes a few seconds for him to pry the panel off with his fingers. As it falls, he begins to reach behind it. I slam my gun hard against his ear. He lets out a howl and slumps over as his hand shoots up to shield another blow.

I don't give him one. I reach in with my left hand and pull out the gun. "This is pretty nice, Mitch. I could give you lots of new assholes with this." I walk around the back of the car to the passenger side and get in. I put the Glock in my coat pocket and keep the .25 in my hand. It may not be as powerful, but I feel more comfortable with it.

"Now stop whimpering," I say, "and make the fucking call. And remember, Mitch: If you try to pull any funny shit, I'll turn you into broccoli. They'll have to spray *you* to keep the bugs away."

The phone rings once before the guy answers.

"Yo."

"It's me," Mitch says.

"What's happenin'?"

"You can drive your date back home now."

"Already? What happened?"

"There's been a slight change of plans."

"What do you mean? Did you get the cards?"

"Yeah, I got the cards."

"How'd you do it so quick?"

"I'll explain later. Meet me where we said. In an hour."

"Why so long?"

"Did you forget what I told you about talking too much on a car phone?"

"No."

"Okay then, just do what I said. Drive the lady home and I'll meet you in an hour. All right?"

"Okay. But dude, you better not be thinking about double-crossing me."

"Don't be ridiculous." Mitch disconnects the phone, shaking his head. "Do you believe that fucking idiot?"

Now that it's safe for me to talk, I shake my head and exhale loudly. "That lousy cocksucker."

"I guess you finally figured out who my partner is, huh?"

I nod. "Now that he's not holding his nose when he talks, it's easy."

"I taught him how to do that. It's amazing how much you can transform your voice"—he presses two fingers to the top of his nose—"just by doing *this.*" His tone changes as he slides his fingers down his nose. "I learned that when I was taking classes at Second City. Pretty neat, huh?"

I nod. "Yeah, Mitch, you're a real fucking comedian."

27

"Now what?" Mitch asks.

"Pull around the corner and park on the block of Hamlin near the old expressway ramp. I want to make sure Frankie gets home safe."

"Don't worry, Phil. Nothing's going to happen to her. That wasn't part of the plan."

"What makes you think I trust that asshole to stick to your plan?"

"He doesn't do anything without talking to me first. But you know, it'll take them a little while to get here. We could save some time by driving over to my bank now. I could take out the money to pay you."

"Just shut up and do what I tell you. I'll have all the time in the world—*after* my wife gets home."

"Whatever you say. You're the one holding the cards."

"That's right. *And* the gun."

He pulls into a parking space a third of the way up the block. I take the keys and put them in my coat pocket. Then I hammer my left elbow into the side of his head.

He lets out a groan and doubles over. He stays like that for a full minute, then comes up glowering. "What the fuck did you do that for?"

I smile. "That was for calling my wife a bitch when I talked to you on the phone before."

He shakes his head, sighs heavily, then stares sulkily ahead. He's got a colorful assortment of bruises forming on his face.

I sit back and light a cigarette. "If your partner's such an idiot, why did you hook up with him in the first place?"

"One reason and one reason only: He's got the connects to unload the cards."

"What about Betty?"

"What, through the store? You got to be kidding. It would take years to sell them. Plus what would Betty's son Jason say when three thousand new cards suddenly show up?"

"Five thousand two hundred thirty-seven," I say. "Frankie counted them."

"Is that right?" He lets out a soft whistle. "I could probably up the payment to twenty thousand if you want."

I smile. "You're not even close to what I want."

"Come on, be reasonable."

I ignore his plea. "So Jason didn't know his father was planning to steal the cards?"

He shakes his head. "He didn't have the first fucking inkling. He's even dumber than his old man."

"So it was just Moony's idea, and then Betty got wind of it and told you."

"Fuck no! It wasn't Moony's idea. It was *my* idea. I planned the whole thing. Moony couldn't plan a goddamn poker game."

"Then how'd he get his money?"

"He married it. Betty had a thing for ball players. She thought she was getting Joe DiMaggio."

"And he thought he was getting Marilyn Monroe."

"Yeah, something like that."

"So where'd you get the idea to pull this off?"

"Moony was always whining to me about this guy Glassner with a shop out in New Jersey—"

"You stayed in pretty close touch with Moony after the Purple Haze closed?"

"Sure." He smiles. "I stayed in touch with Betty, is what I did. The price of doing that was having to listen to Moony."

"He didn't suspect you two were carrying on?"

"Didn't have a clue. The only thing Phil Moony cared about

was collecting baseball cards. Like this Glassner guy. The only reason Moony was willing to rob his shop was because Glassner wouldn't sell him a card he wanted. Moony tried to buy it off him for years, but the guy refused to budge." Mitch grins. "It's on your refrigerator."

"Phil Moony?"

"That's right. His own goddamn baseball card. Which is worth about seven fucking cents. You can't find one anywhere, but it still ain't worth shit." Mitch laughs. "So anyway, I was still in touch with Rio. He was a fucking nut. He'd do anything for money, which is how he ended up in New Jersey. He was doing three years in Rahway prison for robbing a 7-Eleven out there. And I knew he was getting out. So I set the whole thing up. I told Moony it would be a chance to get the old Purple Haze crew back together again. Of course he didn't give a shit about that. All he cared about was getting his goddamn baseball card."

"And so you figured out a way to get rid of both of them. Using me."

"Yeah, that's right."

"Why'd you have to use me?"

"I didn't have to, but why not? It was a chance to reduce my risk. If you don't go along with it, I send someone else to meet Rio and pick up the stuff. If you do, I can get the cards two ways—at your office or at your house. I've got keys to both places." He sighs. "It would have fucking worked too, if that idiot had gotten to your office on time. All he's got to do is hide in there, pop you on the head, and grab the cards."

I nod. It's the same scenario Pat laid out for me, almost word for word.

"Instead he ends up getting into a fucking argument with his sister on the phone and you end up seeing him."

I look at my watch. "Speaking of the asshole, where the fuck is he?"

"Don't worry, he'll be here. Irving Park's a goddamn parking lot with all the construction. He's coming from over near the lake. I didn't want him hanging around the neighborhood in my van. I was afraid someone I knew would come over and start asking him questions."

"You thought of everything, Mitch, didn't you?"

"Almost." He grunts. "What'd I do wrong?"

"A few things."

"Such as?"

"You shouldn't have told me about the Purple Haze. That's how I found out about Rio and the shooting and Little being dead. I also found out there was a guy named Karl Mitchell. So then last night, you left that note on my door, on stationery from 'K. Mitch Michaels.' That's pretty close."

He shrugs. "It's fooled the IRS the last fifteen years."

"The name's what did it. After that, all the little things I should have noticed add up. Like Moony calling when the cops were there and saying he'd call back in an hour. But instead you show up and invite us to dinner, wanting to get us out of the house. And when you find out we're going to be out anyway, you come in and get the briefcase. The final thing was kidnapping Frankie. She wouldn't have let anyone in she didn't know. How'd you get in?"

"It wasn't that easy. I told her I thought I left my keys up in your bedroom last night. Which I did. Intentionally. She didn't believe me at first. She made me wait at the door while she looked. But I slipped in and unlocked the front. I doubt she knows I had anything to do with it."

"It's risky kidnapping someone in broad daylight. But you knew the Miglins were away and the Powells both work. Still you probably would've been better off just keeping her in the house."

He shakes his head. "I wanted you to know we had her somewhere else so you didn't try coming to the house or calling the cops."

"Which one of you guys mixed up the cocktail for Tony Rio?"

"He did."

"Yeah, sure. He made the room reservation, but I'll bet you planted the booze while you were exterminating."

Mitch doesn't say anything, but he looks away from me.

"What about Moony? Did you take care of that or did Betty?"

"Betty. It seemed more natural for her to be at the store in case someone came in."

"When did she find time to put the cyanide back in your garage?"

"What?"

I lift the bag off the floor. "I found it in your garage."

"How the fuck long were you waiting out there?"

"Only a few minutes. Why'd you bother to save it? You weren't planning to pour a drink for your partner, were you?"

A faint trace of a smile forms on Mitch's face. "Now why would I do that?"

I don't answer his question. As I glance in the rearview mirror, I see the Michaels Pest Control van turning the corner to the south of us and coming up Hamlin.

"Get down, he's coming!" I give Mitch a shove to make sure he doesn't do anything stupid. I duck down until the van passes. "I thought you said he'd be coming across Irving Park."

"I thought he would be. He must've taken Grace to avoid the traffic."

We watch as the van turns left at the corner, half a block south of our house. "Where the fuck's he going?" I say.

"Relax, he's probably going to drop her off in the alley."

That makes sense, but I hand him the keys and order him to follow as far as the alley. When we get there, I see that the van has stopped behind our garage.

In a few moments the back door of the van opens and Frankie steps down into the alley. I'm too far away to have a good view of her, but a feeling comes over me that she looks more beautiful now than she ever has before. She turns toward the house and starts slowly toward our garage. As the van pulls away, she doesn't look back. I assume she was told not to. In a few seconds she reaches our gangway and disappears from view.

As a wave of relief flows over me, I get an overwhelming urge to follow her into the house. I want to tell her how much I love her and apologize for causing so much trouble. I want to promise—and really mean it—not to get mixed up in anything so stupid again. But it's not over yet. I'm still mixed up in something stupid. There's a lot of unfinished business to take care of.

"Satisfied?" Mitch asks.

"Somewhat."

"Jeez, I thought you'd be thrilled."

"Listen, cocksucker, don't expect me to be grateful that you didn't kill my wife, because I'm not."

"Okay, take it easy, Phil, I understand."

I tell him to dial my number on the phone. It rings three times, then the answering machine comes on. I'm not surprised. I doubt Frankie feels like talking to anyone. Maybe not even me. But as soon as I start to talk, she picks it up.

"Oh, darling, I'm so glad to hear your voice."

"Are you all right?"

"I'm fine. But I smell like a dead cockroach. I've spent the last two hours in the back of Mitch Michaels' van."

I glance at Mitch and watch a look of surprise spread over his face. Evidently he and his partner didn't consider what a stinkhole his van is.

"He's the one who's behind it all," Frankie says. "He tricked me into letting him in and then—"

"Yes, I know all about it."

"How do you know?"

"It's too complicated to explain now. I'll tell you all about it later."

"When are you coming home?"

"As soon as I can. I've still got some things to take care of."

"Well, hurry."

"I'll try, but it might be a while."

"Should I call the cops about Mitch?"

"No." I glance at Mitch and he lets out a sigh of relief. "Not yet." I smile as his expression sours.

"What about Pat? Do you want me to call him?"

"No. He said he had to go to Wisconsin to see his uncle. Just lock all the doors and don't let anybody in. Nobody, okay?"

"Yes, you can count on it."

"I've got to go now, sweetheart. I love you."

"I love you too, Phil. Be careful."

"I will."

Mitch waits a few moments before speaking. I can't tell if he's being polite or cautious.

"Now can we talk about the cards?"

"What about them?"

"I thought I could buy them from you."

"Fine with me. There's only one problem."

"What's that?"

"I don't have the cards, Mitch."

"What do you mean, you don't have the cards?"

I shrug. "I don't have them."

"Do you know who does?"

"Yeah, I think so."

28

As we approach our destination, I tell Mitch to pull into the alley and park near the gang graffiti on the third garage in from the corner. It's a huge garage.

"You sure the car will be safe here?"

"That's your problem, pal, not mine."

I put the gun into my pocket, but I keep my hand in there in case I need it in a hurry. As we get out, I remind Mitch I've got it so he doesn't get any not-too-bright ideas.

We walk down a gangway on the far side of the garage and stop at the bottom of the cement steps behind a wood-frame bungalow. It's a half-flight up to the door, which leads into the kitchen. Fortunately, I've got a key. This isn't a result of foresight on my part, just my typical combo of dumb luck and laziness. I watched the house three years ago and never returned the key. But I always intended to, so I never took it off my chain.

Peering through the back window, I can see that the kitchen is empty. Down the hall I can make out the dim glow of an overhead light. It's not dark enough to be needed just yet. It could be on to cope with the encroaching dusk, or it could have been left on because no one's home. We'll find out soon enough.

Holding the .25 in my right hand, I turn the key quietly with my left. I twist the knob and give the door a soft push. When it yields, I motion for Mitch to go first.

"Be real quiet," I warn. "This guy shoots first and asks questions later." With his face battered from my contributions,

Mitch's expression carries just enough worry to suggest he might be rethinking his interest in collecting baseball cards.

As we tiptoe through the kitchen, I can hear the sound of running water. The bathroom is at the end of the hall on the right, a dozen or so steps away. The door is open. When we're halfway there, a head leans out, angled in our direction. I'm startled at first because the face doesn't look familiar. But that's because most of it is covered with shaving cream. As the head emerges farther, a hand with a razor comes out with it.

"Hello, Pat," I say. "I hope we didn't disturb you."

He shakes his head as he steps into the hall. A few dabs of the shaving cream drip onto his undershirt and trousers. "No, you didn't disturb me." He motions with the razor. "Hold on a sec, I'll be right with you."

As he starts back into the bathroom, I point the gun and stride toward him. "Stay right the fuck where you are, Pat."

He doesn't raise his hands. He lets the one with the razor fall to his side. He smiles. "You're not going to shoot me, Phil, are you?"

"No, Pat, I'm not going to shoot you. *Unless* you go into the bathroom and try to grab a gun."

"Hell no. I was just going to get a towel to wipe my face."

"I'll get it." I gesture for him to back up and let me by. As I move into the bathroom, I don't see any gun. I take a towel off a rack and hand it to him.

Pat wipes off his face. "So, you want a beer?"

"No, I don't."

"I'll take one," Mitch says.

"Who's this guy?"

"This is my neighbor from across the alley. Mitch Michaels a.k.a. Karl Mitchell a.k.a. Larry Little."

"Oh yeah, the bug man." Pat steps closer to get a better look. "Looks like you stuck your finger up the wrong asshole, Mitch. Or is it Karl? Or maybe I should call you *Lar*. So you're the guy that's been giving my friend so much fucking trouble. Well in that case, you ain't getting a beer."

"Fuck you."

"Ooh, tough talk. Carrying on like that can get your pretty puss remodeled. But I guess you already learned that." Pat turns to me. "What happened?"

"I don't have the fucking time or the interest to tell you."

"Yeah, I understand." Standing, nodding in his undershirt, he suddenly looks very old. "Well I guess you came for the cards, huh?"

"Yeah that's right."

"Have you figured out what you're going to do with them?"

"He's going to sell them to me," Mitch says.

Pat looks at me. "Well, I sure hope you're getting top dollar for them."

The anger and disappointment I'm feeling prevent me from responding. Suddenly I feel very sleazy. Pat still knows how to take the moral high ground, even after he's just double-crossed a friend. I still haven't decided whether to sell the cards to Mitch. All I really wanted to do was get rid of them and get the cops off my back. Now that I've managed to do that, here I am trying to get them back. And I still don't know what I'm going to do with them. I'd like to ask Pat what he thinks I should do, but he's the enemy now. The only thing I know is that I don't want him or Mitch to have them. At least not without paying big-time.

"They're in the front closet. I'll get them for you. You probably want to get going, right?"

"That's right. And you probably have to get going to see old Uncle Jack."

Pat sighs. "I made that up, Phil."

"No fucking kidding."

As Pat starts down the hall, I wave the gun and tell him we're going with him.

"You really don't trust me, do you?" he says.

"No, not one bit."

"I don't blame you."

We walk down the hallway to the front of the house. When we reach the doorway to the living room, Pat moves left to the closet near the front door. He opens the closet door, bends over and pulls out a bulging red tote case with the Winston cigarette logo on it. He shoves it toward my feet.

"For what it's worth," he says, "I was only going to take a few hundred of them. I figured I could sell them and give the dough to Patrick for his tuition. The kid's falling through the cracks on this whole financial aid–scholarship thing. I was going to put them back tonight. That's why I told you to put off the exchange until tomorrow night."

"I didn't have any choice, Pat. They kidnapped Frankie."

"What!" His face goes red, yellow and purple all at once. "Where is she? Is she all right?"

"Now she is. She's back home. But it wasn't easy. I could've used your help."

"Oh fuck, Phil, I'm sorry, I'm really sorry. I know that doesn't mean shit, but I'm sorry. It never occurred to me they'd try and pull something like that."

I shrug and put my gun in my pocket. I'm not going to need it. At least not on Pat. "It's okay, Pat," I say. "You live and learn, right? And I learned something about you. It ain't pretty, but it's good to know. But you want to know what really bothers me? If you wanted to take a piece out of this, help your nephew, whatever, all you had to do was fucking ask me."

He nods. "I know, Phil. I realize I should've done that. But I just couldn't bring myself to do it."

"Come on, what is this—dueling faggots? Let's take the fucking cards and get out of here."

Pat glares at Mitch, who backs up against the wall. As Pat takes a step toward him, Mitch shrinks to about half his size. "You little shitheel. You dare to kidnap this guy's wife for some fucking baseball cards? And then you want to try and hurry us up. You haven't learned a fucking thing yet, have you?"

I realize Pat's overplaying the noble friend role for my benefit, but I also know he's really mad. And the reason I know that is because I know there's one particular thing that gets him that way. It's bad enough that you harm one of his friends, as Mitch did to Frankie, but there's also one particular thing you don't want to say to him. There's one thing you don't ever want to call Pat Ryan, and that's *faggot*. He don't like that. No sir. He don't like that at all.

He reaches out with both hands and grabs Mitch by his shirt collar. If Pat begins hitting him in earnest, things could get very ugly very fast. I don't think we need that right now.

Pat lifts him until they're almost eye-to-eye, leaving Mitch's feet dangling so that only the tips of his shoes touch the floor.

Mitch whimpers as he tries to wriggle free. "Let go of me, goddamn it, let go of me!"

With my attention focused on the two of them, I'm a little slow to respond to the sound of floorboards creaking down the hall. By the time I do, it's too late. R.D. the Artist is standing fifteen feet away. He's holding a gun. I don't know what kind it is, but it's a big one. So big that he's holding it with two hands.

"All right, everybody shut the fuck up and raise your hands! I'll use this fucking thing, I swear I will."

I think about sliding my hand into my pocket but I do as he says. Pat's told me that guys who are smart don't like to shoot guns. R.D. hasn't impressed me as being very smart, but he's certainly outsmarted me. I'm sure he could outgun me too. I decide to let Pat set the tone for how to behave. I'm still pissed at him, but I'm sure glad he's here.

He turns slowly and spreads his hands, tossing Mitch to the floor. This strikes me as a fairly aggressive posture. I wonder if this is when I'm supposed to go for my gun. I don't. If you've got to ask, it's already too late.

"Son of a bitch." Pat shakes his head and looks at R.D. "That was a great fucking act you put on this morning. They should nominate you for a fucking Oscar."

R.D. grins. "Yeah, I thought I did pretty good."

"Careful, Moony's got a piece," Mitch says as he scrambles to his feet and catches his breath. "Two pieces as matter of fact. In his coat pocket."

R.D. glares at me and flexes, as if to tighten his grip. He makes me goddamn nervous. He's got my head in his sight, but he talks to Mitch. "I knew something had to be wrong when you told me to drop the broad off so early. Where are the cards?"

Mitch points. "Over next to Moony. In the Winston bag."

"Well, kick it over here."

To do that Mitch has to go around Pat. He circles warily. I can't tell if he's considering launching a sneak attack or fearful he'll be the victim of one. When he gets even with Pat, he suddenly drops to his knees and lunges for the tote bag. He looks like a dog dodging his shadow.

"Moony, you take off your coat and put it on the floor," R.D. orders. "Do it real slow, with your arms spread and your hands out. Fuck up, and I'll blow your head out onto the street."

This is the moment, I realize. This is the moment when I have to decide whether to be a hero or not. I do exactly as R.D. says.

So does Mitch. He pushes the tote bag down the hallway toward R.D., then pauses on his knees, waiting to take my coat.

"Pass the coat over here too," R.D. says.

"I know that. I'm not an idiot."

"That's open for discussion," Pat says.

Mitch looks up at Pat from his knees and points with his finger. "I should fucking nail your ass, motherfucker. I should fucking nail you."

"Come on, come on, just pass the coat over here," R.D. says. "We don't have time for this grudge shit."

Mitch grips the collar of the coat and gets poised to push it across the floor to R.D.

"I'm glad we finally get to see who's in charge here," Pat says.

Mitch looks up angrily. "What the fuck are you talking about? It was my plan, I thought of it."

"Then why the fuck are you giving him all the cards and all the guns?"

Mitch's eyes go wild as he glances from Pat to R.D.

"Don't listen to him—"

"Fuck you. Who made you boss all of a sudden?" Mitch's hand starts to move down the coat.

R.D. charges forward two steps and thrusts out the gun. "Keep your fucking hands off it!"

I flinch, terrified, certain he's going to shoot. Mitch has the same reaction, only more so. His head is the one R.D. is aiming at.

He covers it with both arms and dives to the floor, sliding past me and into the living room. He ends up sprawled on his gut with his legs sticking out in the hall and the coat twisted under his feet.

R.D. puts on the brakes and wheels around. He looks like a hockey player skidding to a halt right before he reaches the end boards. He loses his balance for an instant, then takes off sprinting down the hall toward the back of the house. By the time it hits me that there's not going to be any shooting, he's already in the kitchen and I'm still standing there frozen.

I shoot a glance at Pat, but he's not going after him. I look down at Mitch, who's trying to pivot on his stomach, fight the coat off his ankles and get to his feet at the same time. It takes him ten seconds just to get to his knees. He grabs the coat by one of its arms as he lunges to his feet. The .25 falls out of the pocket and skids toward the front door. As Pat bends down to grab it, Mitch is finally on his feet. He rocks on his heels, still clutching the arm of the coat. When he sees that Pat has the gun, he recoils and staggers backward into the hallway, away from me. All the while I'm just standing there watching.

Pat lowers the gun and Mitch takes his cue. He turns awkwardly, banging into the wall. He charges down the hall to the kitchen, dragging my coat behind him. When he gets to the back door, he stops and pulls the gun out of the coat pocket. As he pushes the door open, the coat drops to the floor.

I consider starting after him, but Pat puts out his arm to stop me. "Don't even think about it."

"Why not?"

"Let me show you something first." He holds out the .25 with the handle toward me. I take it without saying anything, then watch as he opens the closet door and bends down. When he gets back up, he holds his arm out. In his hand is a large brown shopping bag.

"I don't fucking believe it."

"Believe it," he says.

"What was in the suitcase?" Out in the alley, I can hear a car screeching away. I assume that's Mitch.

"Office supplies. Envelopes, index cards, shit like that."

"You mean you were still trying to hold out on me? What the hell's gotten into you?"

"Do you think I'd let you sell them to that schmuck?"

I'm still pissed, but I feel a grin starting to spread over my face. "What are we going to do with them?"

He shrugs. "I'm sure we'll figure out a way to put them to good use. Right now, I think we should lock the door. I doubt he'll even notice until he's out at O'Hare, but you don't want to take any chances." He starts down the hall, stops and grins. "Boy, would I love to see the expression on that cocksucker's face."

"You and me both."

We're standing there grinning at each other when we hear the squeal of tires. That's followed by the surreal pause that always precedes the unmistakable collision of distant heavy metal. When it comes a moment later, it sounds very close. I flinch. Nine times out of ten with a crash that loud, someone's hurt bad.

29

The human body holds six liters of blood. By the time I get to Mitch Michaels, he's lucky if he has three left. Lose one more, and he's dead meat for sure.

His head is swimming in it, the result of profuse bleeding from the facial cuts suffered when he exited the car by way of the windshield. The seat belt might have done him some good, but whoever heard of a guy in a Corvette wearing a seat belt?

Facial cuts are the least of Mitch's problems. The real leakage is coming from a hole in the right side of his neck that's pumping out blood like a garden hose. I can't immediately tell whether it's coming from the carotid artery or the jugular vein. If it's the carotid, there's no blood going to the right side of his brain. If it's the jugular, there's no blood going back to the right side of his heart. Either way, Mitch is in deep, deep shit.

As I probe with my fingers, I think it's the carotid. Even if he's lucky enough to survive, he'll do so at a severe neurological deficit. Some paralysis is almost certain.

I put my thumb and index finger on the artery and squeeze it tight. That's the only thing I can do. Checking for other injuries is strictly academic at this point. I'm sure he has plenty because he's lying about twenty-five feet from his car. That's a long way to travel even when you don't take the windshield route.

Being that he's unconscious, Mitch isn't issuing any voluntary sounds. But his car alarm is more than making up for his silence. Over my shoulder to my left, four Puerto Rican kids are looking on from beside a very old Lincoln. The nose of their car is pressed in like a bulldog's. The side closer to me consists of little more than heavy-duty plastic secured to the frame with a lifetime's supply of duct tape. That's old damage, probably from last week's accident. The engine is still running, and above the sonic blare of rap music pulsating the whole back end, I can tell the car's in bad need of a new muffler.

One of the kids is screaming to no one in particular as the inevitable gaggle of onlookers starts to assemble.

"Man, I didn't do nothing, man. It wasn't my fault. That crazy asshole pulled right out in front of me."

"Shut that damn thing off!" Even out of uniform, wearing khakis and an undershirt, with his face half-shaved, Pat Ryan still commands immediate compliance as only a cop can.

One of the kids goes obediently to the car and turns the engine off, reducing the noise level by a few hundred decibels. That leaves the incessant wail of Mitch's car alarm as the only major affront to the ears. Pat strides right over to the car and reaches inside. He comes up clutching a fistful of wires and the alarm goes dead.

For a few moments the only sound is the murmur of gawkers letting out their oohs and aahs and telling each other they can't bear to look at all the blood. In my experience, that's never stopped them. The driver of the car starts to plead his case again, but he goes mum as soon as Pat orders him to shut up. Car horns begin honking from traffic backed up down the block, and a few moments later I hear the hallelujah chorus of approaching sirens.

The cops arrive first, two cars converging from different directions. Two of the cops get out and begin directing traffic. Another comes over and asks if I know what I'm doing. I tell him I used to do it professionally, announcing name, rank and engine number. He nods and watches for all of ten seconds, then wanders over toward where his partner is taking testimony from witnesses. Out of the corner of my eye I see Pat intercept him. When they shake hands, I realize this is someone he knows. I'm going to let him do the talking.

By the time the driver finally gets to tell his story before an audience that counts, Mitch's pulse is something that can only be taken on faith. He has as much chance of surviving as the kid does of not getting a ticket. I turn when I hear a familiar voice behind me.

"Okay, Moony, what the fuck've we got?"

I look up to see Ron Ostrow glaring at me from alongside a stretcher. "Looks like a car accident to me, Ron."

"Thanks a whole fucking lot."

"Don't mention it." I slide away to make room for him, still keeping my fingers clamped on the hole in Mitch's neck.

Ostrow moves in beside me to take over. His partner, a young thin black guy I've never met, begins to put shock pants over Mitch's ankles. They're designed to immobilize the legs and keep the body warm. They're a real bitch to get on fat people, but I don't think Mitch is going to present much of a challenge.

"It got the carotid," I say as Ostrow moves his hand down next to mine.

"Yeah, no kidding."

Mitch barely loses any blood as Ostrow and I switch off. That's because his heart isn't pumping much of it. At this point it might not be pumping at all.

"Well, three's a crowd," I say as I get up. "If you need any help, give a holler."

"I think we'll be able to manage all right."

As I scan the crowd, feeling a little dazed, Pat waves for me to come to where he's standing with a pair of cops. One of them is Ted Savage. He's the guy that talked to me when he first got there. The other is named Harv Bennett. I give them Mitch's address and phone number, then Pat begins telling his version of events leading up the accident.

It's an unbelievable story. So unbelievable that they almost have no choice but to believe it. If Pat were lying, he certainly could come up with a better story than this. At least that's what he's hoping the cops think.

He says Mitch and I stopped over for a drink. He was bragging about his new Fiero and Mitch was bragging about his Corvette.

A couple of drinks and the next thing you know, Pat was challenging Mitch to a race.

He speaks in his most sincere seminarian voice. Father Pat, counselor to many, friend to all, bullshitter without equal, amen. "I was only kidding, you know. I didn't expect the guy to take it so seriously. It never occurred to me that he'd take off so fast."

I take up the slack as Pat's voice begins to crack. "It's not your fault," I assure him. "The guy did crazy things."

"He was a friend of yours?" Bennett asks.

"Not a friend, exactly. He was my neighbor."

We pause as Ostrow and his partner load Mitch into the ambulance. There's a sheet over his head. I'm not feeling joyous by any means, but I can't summon any remorse for the guy who arranged the kidnapping of my wife.

"Well," Savage says, looking at me, "I guess someone better call the guy's old lady."

I hold out my hands, which are sticky with blood, and offer a little shake of my head. "She's pretty emotional, I'm not sure I could handle it right now."

Savage sighs. "Do you know any reason why this guy would be carrying cyanide?"

"Cyanide?" I suddenly remember the bag I left on the floor of the Corvette.

"Yeah, that's right. We found a paper bag all ripped up and wet next to the car. There were a couple bottles of booze that were all broken to pieces. There was also a bottle of cyanide."

I shrug. "He was an exterminator."

"Do they use that shit?"

"I don't know."

Savage shakes his head. "Harv, why don't you call the old lady." He looks at us. "You two wait here."

I'm feeling nervous as I watch Savage wander over to confer with one of the other cops. Pat tells me not to worry. In about three minutes, Savage saunters back over.

"All right, you fellas can go now if you want. But we're going to have to get a statement from each of you. Tomorrow will be fine.'' He holds out a business card for me to take. To Pat, he says, ''I take it you still know how to get there.''

''Yeah, I remember.'' Pat nods, then looks at me. ''Let's get back home so you can get cleaned up.''

As we turn away Savage says, ''Hey, Pat, no more fucking races, okay?''

''Yeah, sure thing.''

Back at Pat's house, I wash up and put on one of his shirts. I take him up on his offer of beer, then call Frankie. She sounds frantic to say the least.

''Lydia Michaels just called. She said Mitch was killed in a car accident.''

''I know. It happened on the corner near Pat's house.''

''I thought Pat went to Wisconsin.''

''No, it turned out he didn't.''

''I don't understand.''

''I'll explain it all when I get home.''

''And just when will that be?''

''Half an hour, I promise. Did Lydia ask you to come over?''

''No, her sister's coming, thank God.''

''I love you, Frankie. It's all over.''

''I'll talk to you when you get home.''

I don't like the sound of that.

When I hang up, Pat's holding a shopping bag in one hand and jingling his keys in the other. There's a glove on the hand with the bag in it. ''We should be going,'' he says. ''R.D. could be coming back anytime.'' He holds up the bag. ''And when he does, the cards will be in the last place he'd ever think of looking.''

''Are you going to pick the lock like you did on the one next door to my place?''

''Nah, I think the sucker will come right off its hinges this time.''

''You should stay the hell away from here for a while.'' I don't offer to let him stay at our house, and I know he notes it.

"I intend to. I'll stay away until the cops pick him up."

"Where will you go?"

He shrugs. "Maybe to Wisconsin to see Uncle Jack."

"I thought you made that all up."

"Just that he's sick. The old guy's in better shape than I am. Maybe we'll go over to Kenosha and see the dog races."

As we drive to my office, I ask Pat if he kept any of the cards for himself.

"No. I decided that wasn't such a good idea."

"It's no skin off my back if you do."

"It's skin off mine."

It takes all of five minutes to pull down the door to R.D.'s office. Inside, the place is a nightmare of papers and colored pens and mounting boards.

"Looks like the asshole really is an artist," Pat says as he glances around.

I nod as my eyes fall on a sheet of sketch paper on a corner table with a drawing of a cockroach on it. Under the roach it says, *Don't let him . . . BUG YOU!*

"I think I know how Mitch and R.D. hooked up."

"What's that?" Pat asks, looking over my shoulder.

"It's the logo for Michaels Pest Control."

We stuff the shopping bag into the bottom drawer of R.D.'s desk, right next to a bag of pot. R.D. told me the truth about that. I consider taking it, since my source has suddenly dried up. But I decide to leave it there for the cops. That will be another nail in R.D.'s coffin, albeit a small one.

"I'll make the call to the cops," Pat says as we go down the stairs to the street. "I think I'll give the tip to that nice Miss Washington. That should burn Rosten's ass a bit."

"Just don't call from the phone outside my office."

"Of course not."

I consider stopping by the video store on the way home, but I can't imagine any movie that Frankie would be interested in watching. Instead I ask Pat to pull over at Crown Liquors on Milwaukee. I buy the most expensive bottle of Chianti they have and a fifth of Old Fitz. When I get back in the car, I give the fifth to Pat and tell him not to drink it all in one sitting.

"What's this for?"

"For all your help."

He lets out a snort but doesn't say anything.

"Aren't you going to thank me?"

There are tears welling up in his eyes. "Thank you."

I tell Pat to let me off in front of my house for a change. I don't ask him in, and he doesn't ask to come in. Instead we sit in the car staring at each other.

"I know I shouldn't be asking for favors, but there's one thing I'd really appreciate," he says.

"What's that?"

"If you wouldn't say anything to Frankie about my role in this."

I shrug. "What's there to say?"

"I guess you must think a whole lot less of me now."

"Yeah, I do Pat," I say as I get out of the car. "You're just like the fucking rest of us."

When I open the door, Frankie's standing off to the right in the living room. She's holding the shotgun.

"I hope you didn't hold dinner for me, honey." I try to sound casual.

"Are you kidding? I'm going to hold *this* over your head for the next five years." She raises the shotgun, then stands it against the wall.

I move toward her, smiling. I try to put my arms around her, but she wriggles free and pushes me away. She doesn't wait for an explanation before letting go with a tidal wave of anger. She hits me with everything she's got, so much that I stop counting units of rage when she gets to nine. By the time we reach the dining room, she's got me battered like a piece of driftwood. But I'm so relieved to be home with her again that I barely feel it. Underneath, I can tell she's relieved too. She's putting up a mighty front, but that's all it is—a front. It's like a baseball manager arguing a call when he knows he's not going to win. When the dust finally settles, I ask if she wants to hear the story.

"Of course I do. Over dinner. You're paying."

"Absolutely. Anywhere you want to go."

"Do you feel like a steak?"

I nod. Now I know she's not really mad at me. "I'd love a steak."

"Good, we're going for Chinese."

I hate Chinese food. Even when I use a fork, half of it ends up in my lap. There are only two things I like about Chinese restaurants: mai tais and fortune cookies. A friend of ours says the only way fortunes make sense is if you add the phrase "in bed" to the end of them.

As Frankie opens hers, she breaks into the first smile she's had all evening. " 'You are without equal'—in bed."

"I'll vouch for that," I say.

"You won't be doing any vouching on that subject for quite a while, pal. What's yours?"

I feel a grin spreading over my face as I polish off my drink. " 'You will soon receive an important phone call'—in bed."

"That settles it. I'm getting our number changed tomorrow. And it's going to be unlisted."

Frankie manages to stay mad at me for almost twenty-four hours. That's when I bring home the videos and we go through our reconciliation ritual.

The next day, at Mitch Michaels' funeral, I expect to feel the wrath of another female. I haven't spoken to Lydia yet and I've heard through Frankie that she's very upset with me. But Lydia carries herself with poise and dignity. She's even taken out her curlers for the occasion. When I tell her how sorry I am, she just nods and says she knew Mitch considered me one of his best friends.

It's another woman who takes the opportunity to vent her anger at me, and I'm not prepared for it. As Frankie and I walk to our car after the funeral, a white Lincoln with tinted windows pulls up alongside us. As the front window on the passenger side rolls down, I see Betty Moony peer out at me, designer sunglasses perched atop her forehead.

"You're a rotten no-good son of a bitch, Moony."

I don't have a response ready. But I'm never at a loss for one when Frankie's with me.

"It comes with the name, Betty," she says, shaking her head. "It comes with the name."